THE DOM'S DUNGEON

Cherise Sinclair

VanScoy Publishing Group

The Dom's Dungeon

Foster child. Teenage whore. Now a veterinarian, MacKensie's turned her life around, but the scars remain. She saves her affection for the animals who never judge or scorn her, but it's time to get out, move on from her past in Iowa. So, she arranges a vacation exchange to job hunt in Seattle.

Although the house is lovely, one room is locked. Her years in foster care have given her two 'gifts': a neurosis about locked doors and the ability to open them. After she gets into the room, she's appalled...and intrigued. Chains and manacles, whips and paddles, odd benches with straps...

When Alex returns home days early and finds MacKensie draped over the spanking bench in his locked dungeon, he's furious. But her wariness arouses his protective nature and curiosity, so he strikes a deal to keep her close—she'll act as his submissive in exchange for a place to stay and help finding a job.

He'd planned to use the veterinarian to deter an ex-girlfriend, not *replace* her, but with MacKensie's compelling mixture of strength and vulnerability, the little sub slides right into his well-defended heart.

What reviewers are saying about Cherise Sinclair...

Ms. Sinclair sets the bar for the BDSM erotica genre, especially with her hot dominant alpha males. ~ *The Romance Reviews*

Although I don't use this word often, I certainly will now—*wow*. The Dom's Dungeon is a story that delivers the goods. Fans of this genre have to read The Dom's Dungeon, another hit-the-nail-on-the-head winner by the BDSM Mistress Cherise Sinclair. The writing is superb (as always), the dialogue is both sensual and laugh-out-loud funny, and the characters will remain with you long after you've finished. This is one for the keeper shelf. ~ *Whipped Cream Reviews*

Once again, the exceptionally talented Cherise Sinclair has created an absolutely breathtaking story that will touch both the reader's heart and soul. This author's red hot streak continues with this flawlessly plotted tale filled with vibrant characters and emotionally and sexually charged tension creating a riveting read to enjoy. This author should be at the top of every reader's favorite list! ~ *The Romance Studio*

The Dom's Dungeon

Copyright © 2009 by Cherise Sinclair
ISBN 978-0-9913222-0-6
Print Edition
Published by VanScoy Publishing Group
Cover Artist: April Martinez
~ Reprint ~

Warning: This book contains sexually explicit scenes and adult language and may be considered offensive to some readers. This book is for sale to adults only, as defined by the laws of the country in which you made your purchase.

Disclaimer: Please do not try any new sexual practice, without the guidance of an experienced practitioner. Neither the publisher nor the author will be responsible for any loss, harm, injury, or death resulting from use of the information contained in this book.

Table of Contents

Author's Note

To my readers,

The books I write are fiction, not reality, and as in most romantic fiction, the romance is compressed into a very, very short time period.

You, my darlings, live in the real world, and I want you to take a little more time in your relationships. Good Doms don't grow on trees, and there are some strange people out there. So while you're looking for that special Dom, please, be careful.

When you find him, realize he can't read your mind. Yes, frightening as it might be, you're going to have to open up and talk to him. And you listen to him, in return. Share your hopes and fears, what you want from him, what scares you spitless. Okay, he may try to push your boundaries a little—he's a Dom, after all—but you will have your safe word. You will have a safe word, am I clear? Use protection. Have a back-up person. Communicate.

Remember: safe, sane, and consensual.

Know that I'm hoping you find that special, loving person who will understand your needs and hold you close.

And while you're looking or even if you have already found your dear-heart, come and hang out with the Masters in Club Shadowlands.

Love,
Cherise
Cherise@CheriseSinclair.com

Chapter One

MacKensie slowed the rental car and looked down the curving cobblestoned driveway to the red brick English Tudor house. Surely this was a mistake. But the number on the wrought-iron gate matched the one on the form from Exchanges for Vacations. She drove past a landscaped lawn the vibrant green of the Pacific Northwest and stopped in front of the garage.

Feeling as if someone would call the police on her at any moment, she walked up the steps to the front door. Here was the true test: a keypad. She punched in the number the owner had e-mailed, and her jaw dropped when the lock *snicked* open. *Right place.*

She glanced down at her scruffy T-shirt and faded jeans. *Wrong person.*

A growl at the door announced the reason the owner had picked Mac rather than some other vacation-exchange client. She huffed a laugh. It was probably the first time anyone had ever chosen her for anything. She pushed the door open. "Hey, Butler."

Another growl, a whine. Mac dropped to her knees on the tile flooring, averted her gaze, and held out her hand. "Easy, Butler." His owner, Alex, called him all bluff and no follow-through. He'd damned well better be right. She sure didn't want to start her new life by becoming a dog's chew toy.

In her peripheral vision, she watched the elderly black mongrel inch up to her hand, tail curled under his belly. A scared dog, the most dangerous kind. But oh, the scars on his muzzle and his legs, his ragged ear, told a story of pain. "You've had a hard life, haven't you? Me too. I think we can be buddies, don't you?"

She felt the warm muzzle touch her hand, and she turned slowly. Butler held his ground, his tail still low but starting to wave back and forth. He wanted to be friends so badly. A mixture of Lab and golden retriever, she'd guess, the friendliest breeds in the world. "Yeah, we're good, huh, Butler." She gently scratched his neck and ruffled his fur. He edged close, and the big body started to wiggle.

She laughed, still not moving anything but her hand, slowing her petting and letting him nudge her hand. As they got to know each other, she gave him a quick once-over to make sure there weren't any problems the owner hadn't mentioned. She could do a more complete one later. "But you look just fine and healthy, don't you, Butler?" she crooned. Babysitting him would be a pleasure, not a chore. She gave him a final pat and rose.

Her suitcase weighed a ton and grew heavier as she climbed the stairs. Panting, she stopped on the little landing and ran a hand over the hand-carved railing. *What a place.* Was the owner insane, wanting to exchange this palace for her tiny Iowa house?

On the second floor, she checked out the guest rooms. The owner's information sheet indicated she could take any of them. Tough choice, but the view of the Olympic Mountains decided her on the fourth one. With pale blue floral wallpaper and a cream and blue Oriental carpet on the floor, the room felt very peaceful. With her limited wardrobe of interview clothes and jeans, unpacking took only a few minutes.

Time for a tour of the house. She trotted downstairs and explored what would be her home for the next two weeks. On the west side: a formal living room with a gas fireplace and a traditional den that held an office area, dark leather furniture, and well-filled bookcases. She stopped long enough to check the books. Classics and mysteries. History and historical fiction, with a major emphasis on war. Bloodthirsty guy. No romance books— not surprising—but very little science fiction either. Pretty worthless library. Oh well.

She continued and found a well-appointed kitchen near the back of the house. The east side held a formal dining room and a cozy family room that led onto a patio. Walking back toward the foyer, she noticed a heavy, dark oak door tucked neatly under the staircase. Just like Harry Potter's cupboard, only done with style.

Locked.

Now isn't that odd? The master bedroom hadn't been locked, and neither had the den with all the office equipment, although the oak filing cabinets were. The owner had even left the computer unprotected, with a note taped on the monitor that she could use it if she wanted.

So what was behind this door?

Butler walked up behind her, his toenails clicking on the pale gray tile.

"You're right, guy," she told him. "None of my business. Why don't you show me the backyard?"

Out through the family room to the covered patio and, okay, if she'd fallen into hog heaven, so had Butler, with at least an acre of backyard. Wiggling in excitement, he brought her a ragged ball for her to throw. And throw. And throw. For an old dog, he didn't tire out worth a darn. Finally she called it quits and tossed the ball into a box filled with more throw toys. "We'll get to those tomorrow," she told him.

The uncovered end of the patio had an inground Jacuzzi.

She eyed it. The foster home where she'd been raised hadn't possessed amenities like Jacuzzis, and she sure hadn't had one during her year on the streets. She'd been in a hot tub twice during her college years at Iowa State, none since. Although lots of homes in Oak Hollow had Jacuzzis, once her past had been discovered, the good and righteous townspeople shunned her socially, even if she was good enough to treat their pets. And in all reality, if she hadn't partnered with Jim Anderson in the only vet clinic in town, they probably wouldn't have allowed her to touch their pets.

The familiar bitterness mingled with sadness, and then she brushed the emotions away. Hey, she was here, in Seattle. No one knew her or that she'd been a whore. She could and would start a whole new life.

And that life really should include a Jacuzzi. She eyed the eight-foot brick fence around the backyard. No one could see over that thing. Giggling at her boldness, she stripped right down to her birthday suit.

✧ ✧ ✧ ✧ ✧

Alexander Fontaine strolled toward the security gate at Sea-Tac Airport. *Excellent timing.* He'd left just enough time to clear security before the plane to Des Moines boarded. As he walked, he programmed a reminder on his BlackBerry to check that the veterinarian was doing all right with his dog. Her credentials had been excellent, but Butler had never been impressed by academic awards.

Before he'd finished, the phone rang. He glanced at the screen. *The Seattle Harbor Hotel.* Odd. He thought he'd left everything tied up, at least until he returned.

"This is Fontaine."

"Alex, this is Craig Dunlap. I wanted to check…" The manager of the hotel paused. "Ah, it's about the seating arrangements at the ball."

"Go on." The head table's seating had been set and confirmed weeks ago.

"My secretary had a call from your...from Miss Hanover. She wanted to add a few extra people and rearrange the—"

"Stop." Alex took a breath to cool his anger. Not Dunlap's fault in any way. "Craig, I appreciate your calling to confirm. Please leave the seating arrangements as they are and tear up anything Miss Hanover suggested. Now and in the future."

"Of course, sir."

"I'm sorry for any inconvenience this"—*millstone around my neck*—"lady might have caused. Thank you again for checking."

"My pleasure, sir."

Alex flipped the phone shut, then opened it to check the recent calls. Five from Cynthia. With a grunt of annoyance, he dropped the phone back in his pocket. The woman had passed *persistent* and headed right into *obsessed*. Apparently his plan of escaping her attentions by attending a conference and touring Fontaine holdings in Iowa had been extremely optimistic.

He dodged a woman pulling her bag on a leash, then a gaggle of teenagers. What was he going to do about her?

"No...my bag! Stop!" The wavering voice came from behind him.

Alex turned and spotted an elderly woman frantically trying to rise from the floor. A suitcase lay beside her. The unkempt man sprinting away from her, and toward Alex, had a black purse tucked under his arm like a football.

Anger welled up inside Alex. A man had a responsibility to protect the helpless, not abuse them. This looked like a fine time to do some instruction. He turned away then, just as the thief darted past, and stuck his foot out. The man went down with a satisfying *thud.*

Alex put a foot on the purse strap, figuring the thief would cut his losses and escape. Instead the man snarled. From the whites around his pupils, he appeared higher than a kite. He pulled a knife and sprang at Alex. Alex blocked, knocking the knife to the outside, and punched him hard in the jaw.

Yeah, he was high all right. The thief shook off the punch and charged again, swinging the knife.

Alex started to dodge, but a little teenager ran right between them. Unable to do anything else, Alex grabbed her, spinning her out of the way and taking the knife in the back of his shoulder.

Pain ripped through him in a searing-hot flash. Growling, Alex turned, grabbed the man's knife arm, and side kicked into his stomach.

No reaction. He slammed his foot farther to the left, feeling the bastard's ribs break like kindling. And the guy was *still* on his feet, waving the damned knife. Hell with this. With one savage kick, Alex took out the guy's knee.

PCP or not, nobody walked on a joint that wasn't there. Howling curses, the man crumpled. Unable to rise, he pounded his knife on the floor.

Alex eyed him and considered thumping him one more time just to shut him up. Instead, as blood trickled down his back, he went to help the old lady to her feet and give her back her purse.

"Bless your heart," she said, clutching the purse to her chest. "I don't know what I'd have done if he'd gotten away. I have a new great-grandchild in Ohio, and—"

Airport security arrived then to haul the druggie away, and Alex ended up in the nearest emergency room getting his back stitched up. By the time he finished giving the police a statement, his flight had departed with his luggage on it. Due to a plane being taken out of service, all seating on the next flight was completely filled, with a long waiting list, and the soonest he could reschedule his flight was two days away.

Well, fine. He hadn't wanted to go to Iowa anyway.

Back hurting like hell, Alex got in his car and headed home.

✧ ✧ ✧ ✧ ✧

Mac sprawled in the Jacuzzi, legs floating in the swirling water. As steam rose from the surface, the slight tang of chlorine blended with the fragrant rosebush climbing the house. Bubbles everywhere, taking away the aches of the long flight and the stress of city driving. A slow rain had started a few minutes before, sending down little cold drops onto her exposed shoulders. Maybe she'd died and gone to heaven.

But when she shoved her hair back, she noticed her fingers had turned to pale prunes. No prunes allowed in heaven. Time to get out.

She'd soaked so long, her body radiated waves of heat as she picked up her jeans and shirt. Ugh. Already wet from the rain. She should have left them under the veranda, but with her enthusiasm about getting into the Jacuzzi, she hadn't been thinking. Laughing, she used the damp clothing to wipe herself down before entering the house bare-ass naked. Hey, Butler wouldn't tell, right? Feeling wonderfully decadent, she waltzed through the house, carrying her damp clothing.

By the stairs, she glanced at the locked door. And stepped closer.

No no no, MacKensie, don't touch. This is an obsession. Don't give in. She put her hand on the knob, gritting her teeth when it didn't turn.

It wouldn't open.

The floor shifted under her feet, and she could almost hear a door slamming shut, over and over, like explosions of sound back into her past. Then Arlene would turn the key, shutting her into the tiny space and the awful, monster-filled darkness that seemed to suck away all the air in the room.

Mac's hand turned clammy, slipping on the knob as she heard her foster mother's voice, "*You little demon from hell. You stay in there until you're fit for the light.*" Hours and hours in darkness and fear.

A whine and a wet nose made her jump. "*Frak* me!"

Butler looked up at her with big eyes, tail wagging.

"Sorry, darling." Heart racing, she pulled her hand off the knob to rub his head and whisper, "Your babysitter's a mess." Especially when finding a locked door. In her very own vacation house. Stomach twisting, she fought…and lost.

A pocket in her damp jeans yielded the wallet where her lock picks mingled with the coins. She smiled and pulled two out. An inside door—piece of cake. A trickle of excitement traveled up her spine. She hadn't popped a door open since last year when Old Maude had gotten locked out of her house. Of course, proving she could break in hadn't done her reputation in Oak Hollow any good.

Just open it. That wasn't so bad a crime. Picks in hand, she knelt in front of the door. One pin, a little pressure… *Gently, gently.* The next, rake across it. A simple lock. The door swung open.

Oh yeah. The tightness in her chest disappeared; she could take a deep breath again. The door was open.

She glanced at Butler, who'd sat down to watch her, then at the edge of darkness. Now why had the owner locked the door? "Maybe I should take a quick look, huh, buddy?" *Who knows, maybe the owner left a heater on or something. Can't have the place burning down, right?* Really, just think of it as her duty to a vacation-exchange partner.

She pushed the door open a little farther, and the scent of leather drifted to her. Her fingers found the light switch, and old-fashioned brass sconces on the walls lit with a subtle flickering like candlelight.

Frak me, but what is this? Iron bolts studded a wall of red brick. Manacles dangled from the higher rings, shackles lay on the floor.

The back wall had a big, leather-covered cross with cuffs. A St. Andrew's cross. She not only remembered the name, but she knew what this place was: a dungeon—a private BDSM dungeon. And very well equipped.

Excitement slid across her skin like a cool breeze. The first time she'd seen a BDSM club had been years and years ago when an elderly businessman with a taste for the exotic had hired her for the whole evening. God, the tales of whips and bondage scared her, but her pimp terrified her more. Mac's mouth twisted as she remembered how Ajax had patted her on the head like a dog before shoving her into the man's car.

She'd been prepared for pain. To her shock, the john—the client—made her strap *him* to the cross and beat him with a switch. Hitting him, seeing his skin redden and welts appear, had made her sick inside. But it made him rock hard, and he'd barely lasted a second afterward. He departed, leaving Mac to wander around the club. And then she'd seen a man—a Dom—doing what she'd just done, whipping his sub, only with far-greater skill and...something else. She watched how he controlled his submissive, how he alternated pain with gentle touches. He'd touch the woman intimately and then caress her face before starting again.

Mac hadn't been able to stop watching. She hadn't felt arousal—hell, sex hadn't interested her since her first month as a hooker—but something else.

Later, in college, she'd ventured into a different BDSM club, not once, but twice. But when a Dom had approached her, she'd fled. No one was going to control her, no matter how...interesting it looked. She'd had enough of that to last her whole life.

Her hands hurt. Mac blinked and refocused in the present. *Dungeon. Vacation exchange. Seattle.* Giving a snort of exasperation, she uncurled her fingers where the nails dug into her palms. *Veterinarian, Mac, remember?* Not a whore, not since Jim and Mary had found her broken on the sidewalk. Her own personal angels, and they'd better reside in heaven now or she'd kick God's ass.

After pushing the door almost closed to keep Butler out, Mac slunk in, feeling like a dog herself. A naked alley dog. So a dungeon in the heart of a ritzy, stuffy house. Who knew?

She bit her lip. The owner wouldn't know if she snooped a little, and she could look at everything and actually satisfy her curiosity in a way she couldn't at the clubs.

Afterward she could leave the door unlocked until her vacation ended. Unlocked doors didn't bother her at all.

Maybe she should run upstairs and get some clothes on? Running around like this was...strange. But rather exciting. She grinned and walked across the room.

She tried out the waist-high bondage table, lying on it faceup. Imagining herself in the cuffs and strapped down with someone standing over her gave her a horribly vulnerable feeling...and yet the soft leather seemed to caress her skin. Next she stood against the massive wooden St. Andrew's cross fastened to the wall, remembering the women in the club, hands raised over their heads, legs spread. When her nipples tightened to aching points, she looked around for a source of cold air and found none.

She examined the nasty whips and then slapped one of the multistranded floggers against her leg. It created an odd thuddy sensation, not the stinging she'd expected. The thin wooden cane that she tried next hurt a lot more.

Whoever lives here must be a very scary person. Good thing he's gone.

Finally she came to the one piece of equipment that kept drawing her attention. She circled the spanking thing twice, trying to ignore the needy twisting inside. But just the thought of spanking had always...bothered her. She brushed her hand over the firm leather and felt a tremor of excitement. All right, then. How would a person use this one? It looked an awful lot like a vaulting horse for gymnastics, almost a sawhorse with a barrel shape on top. But no gym vaulting horse boasted leather cuffs on the legs. Littler cuffs on that side and bigger ones here indicated that a person didn't straddle the horse but would lie across the barrel part, head down and butt up.

What would that feel like?

Well, she'd tried everything else in the place. With a tiny giggle, she jumped up and draped herself over the top.

Chapter Two

A lex parked next to the cheap rental in his driveway. Obviously the exchange person had arrived. Had Butler liked her? Finding the woman's mangled remains in the foyer would really top off the day.

Hopefully he could work out some arrangement with her. By the time he could get a flight, the conference would be almost over, so he saw no point in pursuing that plan. Damned if he'd take up residency in some hotel in his own town. She'd just have to see reason. The house was big enough they didn't have to run into each other, or maybe he'd give her enough money to rent a hotel.

He walked in and called, "Hello."

Silence.

Then with a *woof* of delight, Butler appeared from around a corner, skidding on the slick marble tiles in his excitement. Alex chuckled as he petted the squirming beast. They'd lived together for a good five years, ever since he'd found the dog skulking around the garbage bin at the beach house. His mother hadn't been impressed, but dignity ranked high on her list of priorities and was nonexistent on Butler's.

"So where's our tenant?" Alex asked as he tugged gently on Butler's ears. He didn't hear any noise in the house, so she was probably upstairs unpacking. As he headed toward the stairs, he felt a warm trickle from under the dressing the emergency-room nurse had applied. Apparently his stitches hadn't appreciated being rubbed against a car seat. Turning, he headed for the dungeon, where he kept most of his first-aid supplies. Might as well patch himself up, although that might prove difficult, considering the wound was on his back. Maybe he'd grab some gauze and tape and see if he could get the woman to slap it on. She was a vet, after all, which was one of the main reasons he'd chosen her.

He went down the hallway to his dungeon and stopped. The door stood slightly ajar, and he knew he'd locked it before he left. In fact, he'd even checked it before leaving. Anger unfurled inside him, growing hard and fast. The terms of the vacation trade were spelled out clearly in the contract, including the locking of nonessential rooms. She'd deliberately broken in.

He couldn't hear anything inside, but he'd soundproofed the room years ago.

Placing a hand on the door, he silently pushed it open. Not difficult to spot her. She'd draped herself over the spanking bench, head hanging down on one side, legs on the other, with her ass—a pretty, round ass—up in the air.

Well, well. A trickle of humor dampened the anger. Now wasn't that an appropriate position for someone richly deserving punishment?

He'd enjoy turning those cheeks a nice pink.

He walked over silently. Before she could move, he set his hand on the back of her neck, holding her firmly across the horse. She gave a yelp of surprise. Her thick, wavy golden hair hung almost to the floor, concealing her face. Maybe five-five or so, she had a nicely toned body.

Since he'd adjusted the horse for Cynthia's taller body, this smaller woman's arms and legs dangled, giving her no leverage to struggle. Although she was certainly trying.

He didn't bother to listen to the sputtering and cursing coming from the submissive under his hands. And that she was submissive, he had no doubt. Someone might have played on the spanking horse, possibly, but the way she'd positioned herself so carefully, and the tiny wiggle she'd given when finally in position, spoke of a person imagining herself helpless and being excited at the idea.

A Dom had a duty to give a submissive what she needed, not always what she wanted…and to administer punishment as required.

"I locked this room before I left. You broke in." A sub always needed to know the reason for the punishment. He gave her a hard swat, precisely placed on the fullest part of her buttocks.

What is the owner doing home? A second later, the man's hand hit Mac's bottom, the stinging pain almost extinguished by her shock. *He hit me!* She struggled furiously, but his large hand gripped her neck and pressed down unyieldingly.

Naked and caught. Humiliation swept through her in a hot wave. "Let me go!"

He didn't respond to her struggles or shouts, as if what she said was meaningless. His voice deep and controlled, he said slowly, "I trusted you with my house and my dog. Rather than respecting that, you break into a locked room and make yourself at home. Your punishment is five swats." His hand slammed across her bottom again.

And again.

The burning pain swamped her mind. The fiery sensations on her bare skin hit each time in the same spot. At the fourth blow, her eyes filled with tears. His hand felt hot against her neck as his grip on it eased slightly. From deep inside her, guilt and shame welled up, choking off her yells. She shouldn't have opened a locked door; she'd betrayed an agreement, a trust.

But spanking? No one had ever spanked her. Ever. Foster children got time-outs; children who belonged got spanked.

As he gave the final swat, a shudder ran through her, leaving her trembling inside and out.

He still held her firmly with one hand; now the other stroked down her back, a firm, knowing touch. Not sexual but...assessing. When the hand reached her stinging bottom, she hissed with the increased pain.

"I want you to remain in this position—what was your name?—ah, MacKensie. Is that clear?"

"Yes." She couldn't manage more than a whisper as the magnitude of her terrible blunder struck her harder than his blows. *Oh God, what have I done?* She'd not only broken the Exchanges contract, but more... Her neurotic need to open doors had destroyed her new start. How could she get a job as a vet out here if he turned her into the police? Or he could do something worse...

After Exchanges sent Fontaine's bio, she'd checked him out on the Net. He was not only richer than God, but he mingled with the elite in Seattle society. He could easily destroy her reputation. Who would hire her if he denounced her?

Footsteps moved away and returned. Then his hand pressed down on the small of her back. "This won't feel good, but it will help the pain and redness." She had only a second to wonder what he meant before he began to massage lotion into her skin, right where he'd hit her. As pain flared back to life, she jerked, arched, tried to kick—and got a swat on her burning butt.

"Lie still." The sheer authority in his voice made her force herself back down. "Good girl." His touch gentled, and the pain eased, leaving only a hot throbbing in its wake. "Up you come now." He lifted her off the bench. Broad hands gripped her upper arms, steadying her when she wobbled.

After a breath for courage, she looked up into a strong face and piercing blue eyes. His short dark brown hair lightened to gray at the temples. He had sharply chiseled features and a stern jaw with a cleft in the chin. A white, tailored shirt with sleeves rolled up displayed muscular forearms.

Still holding her by one arm, he cupped her cheek, using his thumb to brush away her tears. "Almost over, pet," he murmured, then stepped back. "Kneel and apologize." His voice had turned cold, eradicating for a frozen moment even the thought of arguing.

But *kneel?* Did he think he lived in some feudal century or— her mind flashed to the BDSM clubs she'd visited and the submissives at their master's feet. Frak, she'd not only found the Dom's dungeon, but she'd found the Dom to go with it.

Still…if this guy thought she'd kneel, he could think again. She gave him a scathing look and headed for the door. Could she arrest him for hitting her? Probably not, considering she'd broken—

"MacKensie."

She glanced back.

He crossed his arms over his chest. "If you leave, I'll report this through legal routes. If you stay, perhaps we can discuss alternatives."

What kind of alternatives would a man demand? Oh she knew exactly what, and a cold hand squeezed her chest. She wouldn't be a whore again. Never. But stalling couldn't hurt. Maybe his anger would cool a little. "What alternatives?"

He pointed at the floor in front of him. "Apologize."

Fine. She started back across the room and almost groaned when the room blurred. No food since breakfast, too long in the Jacuzzi, and this… Her legs buckled as she tried to kneel, and she landed painfully on her knees. She gritted her teeth against the pain.

He bent over and lifted her face. "Are you all right?" he asked softly.

She nodded, confused. *Beat me and then make sure I didn't hurt my knees?* Was the man bipolar?

After caressing her cheek, he stood. And waited.

Damn him. She forced the words out, the taste of the apology bitter in her mouth. "I'm sorry. I shouldn't have opened a locked door." She stopped.

"'Please forgive me, Sir,'" he prompted.

Oh honestly. Her hands tightened into fists. If she thumped him in the balls, she could run and... And what? Escape onto the street bare-ass naked? Assuming her legs even held her up, because right now that wasn't looking likely; she could feel fine tremors sweeping through her. "Please forgive me, S-sir." Her voice broke at the last word.

"Very nice." He paused. "You have my forgiveness."

Relief swept through her so powerfully that she shuddered. Now if he'd just let her leave.

He walked across the room—maybe she should make a dash for it?—and returned. A warm, incredibly soft blanket wrapped around her.

She pulled it closer and pushed to her feet—too quickly. Cold sweat broke out on her skin, and a hum filled her ears. She took a step and squinted, hoping to see a chair. *Sit. Must sit. Not faint.* Her legs gave out.

He scooped her up as if she weighed nothing. Shifting her in his arms, he winced and said under his breath, "Damned knife," then pulled her against his chest. Carrying her. No one had ever carried her. Ever. Even when she'd been little. Her foster mother hadn't believed in coddling children.

She didn't even feel unsafe being held so high. His chest was solid muscle, his arms like iron bars under her shoulders and legs; the world probably would end before this man dropped her. He walked over to a chair she hadn't noticed in the corner of the room and sat down.

When her weight landed on his thighs, her butt burned, and she jumped. What in heaven's name was she doing? "Let go of me." As she pushed against his chest, the blanket dropped away from her, baring her breasts. Dammit.

"I'll let you go when I know you can walk across the room without passing out." His arm tightened, keeping her in place. When his hand rose, she forced herself not to cringe. Her fingers curled into claws to rip him apart if he tried to grope her.

He huffed a laugh. "Quite the little cat." His hand slowly lowered to stroke her hair with a disconcertingly gentle touch. "Gently, pet. Take a minute to get your bearings. Then you can get dressed. And we'll talk."

Oh, she heard a definite threat in that last phrase. But as the warmth from the blanket and his body sank into her, her muscles melted as if the trembling had used up all her energy.

He leaned back in the chair, settling her more comfortably. "Tell me. Has anyone ever spanked you before?"

"No." Her cheek rested against the softness of his shirt. She could hear the even thud of his heart under her ear; her pulse still raced twice as fast. "Never." And it would never happen again. Yet the memory of his hand holding her in place, the feeling of being overpowered, made her feel weird. *Lost.*

"Have you been around BDSM before?"

She tried to push away, and he eliminated her struggle to move before it hardly began. She glared at him.

"No, you're not getting up yet," he said. "I want to see some color in your face first."

Her teeth ground together, but she wasn't totally stupid. The little flickers of blackness at the edge of her vision and the numbness around her lips and fingers said he was probably right. She'd pass right out before she got to the door, and wouldn't that be the perfect end to this disaster? She pulled the blanket tighter and prepared to wait him out.

His scent surrounded her, a rich blend of exotic cologne and masculine fragrance that blended with the scent of leather. His voice deepened. "MacKensie, have you been around BDSM before?"

"I went into a club three times."

"Ah." Alex felt an odd satisfaction at her answer, almost as much as he felt holding her in his arms. One visit to a club, maybe two, he could attribute to curiosity. A third time? Probably she'd discovered a need that BDSM satisfied...or might satisfy.

He shifted her so he could see her face better. She was a sweet armful, curved in all the right places. Her big brown eyes were darker than Butler's but could hold the same pleading look, one that pulled at his heart and a Dom's need to make things right. Everyone had hidden places and dark secrets, but this little vet's eyes held something shadowy and sad. "What did you do when you were there?"

"Nothing."

That didn't seem right. She had a prettiness and a vivid energy that would definitely attract a dominant. "Didn't any of the Doms come over and meet you?"

A slight nod and her shoulders moved in a shrug.

"Then you were the one to tell them no. Why?"

Eyes going cold and blank, she stiffened and tried to get off his lap again. His questions had obviously probed into something painful, and she retreated rather than attack. Why? What in her past could shut this spitfire's emotions down? He felt a tug inside himself, a need to help.

"I'm fine now. I need to go pack," she said, still pushing at his chest.

Her color had mostly returned, and the tremors shaking her body had diminished. He had no reason to hold her further. He grasped her around the waist and set her on her feet, enjoying the flash of her rose-tipped breasts before she recovered the blanket. But he shoved his normal male reaction back down. This interlude with MacKensie had been about discipline and then aftercare. Sex shouldn't and didn't enter into it.

He glanced at his watch, then her. "You have ten minutes to change. Then I will meet with you in the family room for our discussion."

Her brown eyes kindled delightfully, but after a cautious look at his face, she simply nodded and headed across the room. Quickly.

Butler sat just outside the door, whining as MacKensie picked up her clothing. And although shaken, and her ass undoubtedly hurting like hell, the woman stopped to pet Butler on her way past.

Alex frowned. He'd thought to simply kick her out of his house and notify Exchanges that she'd broken into a locked room. But now... He rubbed his jaw. She didn't quite add up. The way she'd flared up at him indicated a feisty personality, and her instinctive responses to command indicated a penchant for submission, but although pleasing, the combination wasn't that uncommon.

No, that underlying vulnerability that she'd so quickly hidden drew him. And when she petted Butler, he could see a pure sweetness under her defenses.

He'd see what came of the discussion, but she'd roused his protectiveness. Discipline and punishment could be a two-way street. She'd been taken under a master's will, but in turn, he'd received her submission, and with that, a bond between them had been created.

Just what I need, another submissive.

Chapter Three

P anting from her dash up the stairs, MacKensie entered her bedroom and locked the door behind her. Not that there was much point since the guy probably had a key to every room in the house.

The bastard.

In the bathroom, she tossed her clothing into the bathtub. It landed with a wet *splat.*

She glanced in the mirror and rolled her eyes at the vision of beauty: face dead white, hair in tangles, tear streaks. Then again, she should look at the bright side; if she'd worn makeup, her mascara would have been all over her cheeks.

The bastard.

Speaking of which. She dropped the blanket and turned to check her backside. Fiery red handprints marked the white skin of her bottom. Her teeth ground together as another wave of shame ran through her.

He had no right to do that…

She touched her butt carefully, hissing a little at the sting. To her surprise, she saw he'd left no welts or bruises, and she realized he hadn't been totally brutal. His grip had been firm enough to hold her and had eased when she stopped struggling. No, he'd administered a carefully controlled spanking, and somehow that made him scarier than an out-and-out brute.

Didn't matter. She wasn't staying, and she didn't have time to wallow in self-pity. After rinsing the sweat and tear streaks off her face, she dragged on a T-shirt and jeans, then repacked her suitcase.

I am so out of here. And then what? Mac closed her eyes as worries piled higher and higher like thunderclouds before a storm. Worries that all started with the letter *m* for money.

Obviously she should have sold the house Jim had left her before coming here. She huffed a laugh. Face it. She'd been too insecure to put all her eggs in the Seattle basket; she hadn't wanted to give up the house until she knew she had a job.

But her lack of confidence had screwed her up now. She had no money, dammit. After paying funeral expenses, she'd barely managed to scrounge up enough money for the airfare and car rental.

She couldn't—wouldn't—ever regret helping Jim before he died. Nothing would ever repay what he and Mary had done for her; what were money and time? Her eyes burned with tears. What she wouldn't do to have them back again.

But they'd packed up and moved to heaven, leaving her all alone…and really, really broke. She'd thought she'd gotten such a lucky break to get to stay in this house while she looked for a job. Before leaving Iowa, she'd lined up interviews with vet clinics for the next two weeks, but now she had nowhere to stay and no money for a hotel room. Maybe she could sleep in her car? But since she didn't own a cell phone, she'd used the phone here as her contact number.

She'd so looked forward to moving to Seattle and starting a new life where no one knew her. A life surrounded by animals that gave back every bit of the affection they received. Being a veterinarian was the best job in the world…if she could find a position.

Fontaine had said he'd discuss alternatives to the legal route. What did he mean by that? If she sneaked out, would he really report her? Would he try to keep her from getting a job? She eyed the antique furniture, the leaded glass panes in the window, the Oriental carpet. Money. And money meant power. He could probably keep her from getting any job in the area with just a word.

Maybe she could go somewhere else? Only that might prove difficult. She closed her eyes, thinking of the hours she'd put in researching the clinics here, applying for jobs, sending out résumés, and setting up interviews. She could do all that again…if she had a phone, her computer and printer, and time. To try to accomplish all that from the back of a car, with no food or phone or money?

Desolation hit, sucking her down into the depths, and then she fought back out. Blinking back tears, she put her chin up and firmed her mouth. *"No retreat; no surrender."* She'd manage, dammit; she always had. Picking up her suitcase, she glanced around the room and saw no trace of her presence.

Once downstairs, she set her suitcase in the foyer and headed for the family room.

"MacKensie." Alex appeared in the door of the bathroom. Shirtless. Her eyes widened at the sight of his bare chest. "Excellent timing. Come here, please."

Coldness swept through her.

He waited.

She hesitated, then realized his face wasn't flushed with lust. She chanced a quick look lower; he wasn't hard. "Excuse me?" *Be polite but stay out of reach.* She straightened her spine and marched forward to stand in front of him. "What happened to the discussion in the family room?" *With you fully dressed.*

"Soon. First, I have a favor to ask of you."

She hadn't been wrong about him after all. Here came the proposition. "What?"

He huffed a laugh. "Such a suspicious mind. Little vet, can you handle the sight of human blood?"

Not waiting for her answer, Alex led the way into the bathroom, letting the bloodstained bandage on his back speak for itself. After a second, she followed him in.

As he handed her the first-aid kit he'd brought from the dungeon, his eyes narrowed. That blank look, like a human whiteboard wiped of emotion, had returned the minute she'd seen his bare chest. She definitely had a problem. Noting a sub's responses was as automatic as breathing to a Dom, and her reaction to being punished—and to him—had been equivocal. Her quite understandable fury had also included an unmistakable need to submit. But the blank look, like the one she wore now, hadn't appeared until he'd asked about why she'd run from a Dom. He angled himself so he could watch her face in the wall mirror as she worked.

When she eased the thick gauze dressing off his back, she frowned. "How in the world did you get a cut like this?"

"I had an altercation at the airport. He had a knife."

Life returned to her face as she cleaned the wound with efficient, easy movements. She obviously didn't have a problem with blood or with touching a man in a nonsexual way. She glanced at him in the mirror, a trace of humor in her eyes. "Since you're still breathing, I assume you won?"

Alex grinned. "I'm not sure I'd call it a win. Although he's behind bars, I missed my flight. My luggage is on the plane. I couldn't book another flight for two days." He shook his head, ignoring the pain as she worked on his back. "There didn't seem to be any point to going to my conference."

"Well, that explains why you came back." She applied antibacterial ointment to the stitches and re-covered the wound with gauze. "I sure wasn't expecting anyone to walk in." This time when her eyes met his in the mirror, her face turned a pretty pink.

He watched and saw her fingers tremble as she applied tape to the gauze. Her gaze followed the line of his shoulder, paused on his bicep—she was seeing him as a man, not a patient. Her color deepened. *Arousal. Aversion.* The little sub had conflicts.

With an audible breath, she stepped back. "All done. Keep it dry and have someone put a clean dressing on it tomorrow."

When he turned and leaned against the sink counter, her gaze dipped to his bare chest. He stood close enough that he could see the tiny pulse in her neck grow more rapid. "Thank you, little vet," he murmured. "You have gentle hands."

"You're welcome."

When he brushed his fingers along the delicate line of her jaw, she stiffened, obviously fighting not to step back. And yet her pupils dilated slightly. Fear and desire, like an abused puppy that wanted to be petted yet cannot trust.

"Let me put on a clean shirt, and I'll meet you in the family room."

She backed up a step, gave him a nod, and headed for the door. In the stiffness of her spine and the ungraceful movement of her legs, he could see the control she exerted not to flee, like a little cat pretending not to notice a Great Dane in the next yard.

She was smart. Sweet. Terrified.

And not his problem, dammit.

Upstairs, he picked up a T-shirt, winced at the thought of pulling it over his head, and then chose a casual button-down instead. Odd how MacKensie's references all praised her character, dedication, and skill. Nothing had hinted at her being the type of person to break into a room. And when she'd apologized, he'd seen not only embarrassment but shame.

But if she were so innocent, how had she managed to get the door open?

He frowned and leaned against the dresser. Interesting conundrums. What did a Dom owe to a sub not under his command? She obviously didn't want to stay here, and problems or not, her choices were her own.

But what about Exchanges? He needed to notify them about her behavior. And he had a certain responsibility to the animals and veterinarians in this community. Could she be trusted?

Yet he'd completely destroy her career if he voiced those questions. Dammit, he didn't know enough to—

His cell phone rang, jarring him from his thoughts. He flipped it open. "What?"

"Oh, Alex, you sound so angry." Cynthia's rich voice poured out like syrup.

The day just got better and better. He should have checked the number. "Cynthia, we're done. Stop calling me. I won't see you or talk to you."

She laughed lightly. "You're my master, so I'll obey and get off the phone now. But I know you'll see me again. You aren't with anyone else, and I know you never go long without a woman. There's something between us, Alex, and I'll wait for you. I'll wait just as long as it takes."

He heard the sound of a kiss, pulled the phone away, and cursed. This was worse than he'd thought.

Hell. He could denounce her in public and humiliate her. He sighed. He not only couldn't do that to a woman, but Cynthia happened to like being humiliated.

"*You aren't with anyone else.*" He could fix that at least. Pick up a sub from the club and—he grimaced—probably end up with another problem. Here he'd thought Cynthia a good choice since, with her wealth, his money wouldn't be a draw.

As he tucked his shirt into his pants and the movement pulled at the tape on his back, he stilled, remembering the little submissive who had applied the dressing. Maybe one simple solution would solve all his problems.

✧ ✧ ✧ ✧ ✧

Mac waited by the door of the family room, relieved when she heard Fontaine's footsteps approaching. It had taken him long enough.

He nodded to her as he entered the room. After crossing to the tiny bar, he poured a glass of wine and then tilted his head, asking silently if she wanted some.

She shook her head. This was no social occasion.

He picked up his glass and moved over to flip a switch on the fireplace. Flames sprouted under the logs, then caught, and within a minute a fire blazed, giving off both heat and a false sense of comfort.

Why was he bothering with all this?

He took a seat in one of the dark leather chairs. Leaning back to watch her with an unreadable gaze, he held his glass of red wine in one big hand, his lean fingers gentle on the delicate crystal.

Mac frowned. Those hands on her body hadn't been gentle at all. Time to get this over with and get out of here. She held her head high and marched forward. "Mr. Fontaine," she said in a cold voice, stopping in the middle of the room.

His lips quirked. "'Alex' will do for now."

For now? What did that mean? "Once again, I'm sorry for my actions. The room upstairs is clean, and I'll just get out of your life now." The thought sent anxiety like ice trickling down her spine.

"Sit down."

"Listen, I—"

He pointed to the chair across from him.

She walked to the chair, a little startled at her compliance. Her usual reaction to an order was defiance, not obedience. When her tender butt made contact with the cushion, she sucked in a breath. A glint of amusement appeared in his eyes. If she could have laid hands on anything throwable, she'd have heaved it at him. "What do you want to talk about?"

His fingers rubbed his lips as he studied her, in no hurry to answer her question. In fact, he appeared totally at ease in this awkward situation.

Another reason to hate him. She might be a confident vet, but in social situations she bumbled around like a badly trained puppy. Turning her gaze away, she held her clammy hands out to the fire and then realized how badly her fingers shook. *New plan: fold hands in lap, lean back in chair, meet the man's eyes, and be polite. Piece of cake.*

"The information from Exchanges stated you wanted to trade places to save money while you job hunt," he said finally. "I have the impression that leaving my home might prove more than just an inconvenience for you."

Her breath caught at the accurate blow. She laced her fingers together. "That's not your problem," she said stiffly. But God help her, it was hers. All those interviews that she'd set up. Several clinics still needed to call her with dates and times. "If someone calls… Um… Tomorrow I will call and give you a number… Could you please…" Her voice trailed off. How could she ask him for anything?

"I could, perhaps, be persuaded to let you stay here with me," he said softly.

Her eyes closed as nausea whirled inside her. For a moment, one horrible moment, she actually considered giving in to his pressure tactics. *Tacky motel rooms and dark alleys. Being used.*

She rose. "Forget it. I'm not a prostitute." *Never, ever again.*

His shrewd gaze dropped from her face to her fisted hands. "MacKensie," he said in an even voice. "I've never paid, traded, or bargained to have sex with a woman. I'm too old to start now. Sit down." The command had a touch of the whip this time, and her knees dropped her in the chair before she had a chance to think.

She rubbed her hands on her jeans and frowned. If he didn't want sex with her, then what did he want? And why did his voice give her quivers inside?

"So?" she managed to say, striving for a hint of defiance and failing miserably.

"You need a place to stay during your interviews." His eyes seemed too blue, too intense. "Am I correct?"

How much did she want him to know? Would admitting this make her more vulnerable? "It would be useful," she ventured.

Elbows on the arms of the chair, he steepled his fingers, contemplating her over the top. "I have a problem with just letting you go and not warning Exchanges or the community about your behavior. And I don't know you well enough to assure myself it won't happen again."

Oh no. The iron in her spine started to fold. All her worst fears…but why had he said *persuaded?* "So you suggest what?"

"An exchange of sorts. I would let you stay here, and unless you prove to be untrustworthy, will not speak about your behavior."

"What do you get in return?"

"Let me explain. Over the past month, I took a submissive to a few parties and a BDSM club and then stopped calling her. She apparently has become…fixated on me, and nothing I've said has deterred her. She feels that since I haven't taken on anyone else, it's just a matter of time before I return to her. I think if I appear to be in a relationship, she will give up and move on."

Mac stared at him in disbelief. Rich, handsome, exuding a power that should have women buzzing around him like flies. "You want a girlfriend?"

His deep laugh went through her skin and squeezed her chest. "Absolutely not. I want the *appearance* of a girlfriend. A submissive lover, to be exact."

"Me?"

He nodded. "Perhaps we can solve our problems together in this way."

"No way." She shook her head. *What a horrifying thought.*

"You have an interest in BDSM."

"No, I don't," she said automatically.

His brows drew together, and his blue eyes darkened as if a rain cloud crossed the sky. "MacKensie, the first thing a sub learns is not to lie to her Dom."

"I'm not your sub." Just the thought sent chills through her. She'd seen the way the Doms in the clubs treated their subs, handling them as if the subs had no say over their bodies. She shivered. This man would be no different. Yet she could still feel his arms around her, how he'd held her against him.

"The thought of being my sub appears to frighten you," he murmured, "as well as arouse you."

"Right," she said sarcastically. Like she even knew what arousal felt like? Sex was always for the guy, not the girl. She scowled when his gaze dropped to her chest. "That's not true."

"You may not want to acknowledge it, but your body is interested. And aroused." As if aiming a pistol, he pointed a finger at her chest.

She glanced down at her tits and frowned. Under her thin bra and T-shirt, her nipples blatantly poked out. *Aroused? Me?* And yet her body did feel different, as if her skin had become more sensitive all over. *This is just not happening.* "I'm not going to have—to fuck you. Forget it."

He leaned back in his chair and took a sip of wine, reining in his overpowering presence and giving her a chance to breathe. "Ah. You're uncomfortable with the idea of sex. Perhaps we can work around that. What if"—he smiled slightly—"no fucking were involved?"

"Let me get this straight. I'd follow you around, looking all wussy—with no sex—and you'd let me live here for the next two weeks and wouldn't destroy my reputation."

One eyebrow tilted up. "Nicely put. However, I'd expect true submission from you, MacKensie." He rested his forearms on his thighs and pinned her with a stare. "That's quite different from being wussy. That's giving control to me—control over everything for certain occasions."

The room felt awfully hot, and her heart raced as if she'd run laps for an hour. "What occasions?"

"When at my club. At any party I take you to. Whenever we're with my friends."

Not all the time, then. Could she let him boss her around for two or three hours? With sex out of the picture, this might be doable. A trickle of hope eased the tightness of her stomach. But all that control. She tried to remember what had happened in the BDSM clubs. *Oh frak.* "No whipping or any of that stuff, right?"

He leaned back. "I have a list we'll go through together. But I will expect you to bend over backward to please me, so unless there's something on it that is past your endurance..."

With a mighty yawn, Butler stood up and wandered over to sit next to Fontaine's feet and laid his big head in the man's lap. Mac watched as the lean hands ruffled the dog's ears, scratched under the collar, and then stroked Butler's side. The dog's tail thumped against the floor.

She frowned, feeling a tug at her heart and a decrease in her wariness. Could anyone who loved that ugly mutt be all bad? *Don't be stupid, Mac.* Even mass murderers adored their pets. And yet... No sex, her reputation undamaged... Ack, her reputation. Dear Lord, she couldn't do this.

"What?" he asked, even though she hadn't said anything.

"I plan to start a life here, work here. Being your...whatever... It's too... I can't afford to damage my reputation." And God, she knew how important that was.

"Ah. A fair concern." He nodded. "I will not ask you to"—his flashing grin was devastating—"act as my *whatever* anywhere except with a few discreet friends or at Chains, which is a private club.

Anonymity is part of the contract, and the members value their reputations."

Well. But could she really do this? "A trial period?" she offered.

He nodded. "Fair enough. Tell you what. If you do a really fine job and Cynthia gives up, I'll make some calls and shove some influence your way."

Oh sure, like Mr. Big Shot would know the vet community. "Thank you," she said politely.

Chuckling, he rose. He gave her his hand and pulled her to her feet. "The foundation I oversee helped start both of the county's no-kill shelters and the city's feral-cat program. Once a year we sponsor a fund-raising dinner and dance to benefit all the pet charities in the area. As it happens, the dance is in two weeks, and just about every vet in the city attends."

Her mouth dropped open. This was just what she needed. Oh God, could this possibly work?

Chapter Four

She'd planned to leave the house early the next morning before Mr. Fontaine—Alex—came down to breakfast. But when she walked into the kitchen, she realized from the smell of coffee and the cup in the dishwasher that he'd already been there and gone. Maybe he felt the same need to escape that she did.

Oh that would be the day. She rolled her eyes. That man wouldn't run from anything. Nope.

As she made a fresh pot of coffee, she breathed in the heady fragrance of the aromatic grounds. No cheap coffee for this household. A few minutes later, she poured herself a nice full cup and walked into the sunny breakfast nook. Skirting the antique table and chairs in the center of the room, she chose the couch under a window with a magnificent view of Puget Sound and the mountains turning pink with the rising sun.

When she sat, her still-tender bottom touched the cushions, making her squeak, then scowl at the unwelcome reminder of yesterday.

What a mess. And she'd created it all by herself. She thudded her head on the back of the couch: *dumb, dumb, dumb.* How could she have been so lacking in morals? God, she would never, ever open a locked door again.

But how that man had the nerve to spank her, she didn't know. And then he'd pretty much blackmailed her into cooperating with him. Done a good job of it too. She'd spent most of last night going over her predicament and hadn't discovered any way out of it. With his connections, he could help her secure a job—or could sink her just as easily.

It was the submissive stuff that really sent a chill creeping up her spine. She'd spent enough time in the BDSM clubs to know some of what went on. How could she possibly trust this stranger to…to tie her up or to… Then again, he already had, hadn't he?

He'd had her at his mercy on that bench. Frowning, she took a sip of coffee. In her opinion, spanking her had been way over the top, but considering he'd found her exploring his private dungeon, maybe he'd figured she deserved it. Yet despite his fury and all the nasty whips and floggers and canes available on the wall, he'd contented himself with five swats from his bare hand.

"*Five swats.*" The memory of his voice made a shiver run up her spine. But the man hadn't groped her or done anything remotely sexual, despite her nakedness. Her breath eased out, and her muscles relaxed. Maybe…maybe this would work.

Toenails clicked dully across the marble tile floor of the sunroom, and then Butler trotted over to her, his tail wagging furiously. He put a big head on her knee and gazed at her in adoration.

"Good morning, sweetie." She sent the dog into ecstasy by scratching his sides. "Did you sleep with the brute last night?"

"Actually, the brute makes him sleep in his dog bed on the floor." Alex strolled into the room, holding a cup of coffee, and sat down on the other end of the couch.

"I—"*Good going, Mac.* "I'm sorry. Um. Am I supposed to call you something like 'Master' or something?" *Something totally wussy?*

He chuckled. "MacKensie, there will be times I expect you to be in a submissive role. Certain private parties, at the club, and occasionally at other times if I have friends over who are in the lifestyle. Otherwise we will operate on a fairly equal footing."

"Fairly equal?" she asked carefully.

He had a dimple in his cheek when he smiled. "From what I've seen, you probably aren't submissive twenty-four hours of the day, just under certain circumstances. Of course, that may change as you find out more about yourself." He drank some coffee and stretched an arm across the back of the couch, far enough that he could finger her wavy hair. He didn't touch her exactly, just her hair, and yet there was something intimate, almost possessive, about his action. "Now, aside from this being my house, it happens that I'm a dominant; I like my own way. So we will undoubtedly butt heads now and then."

Well, knowing he really didn't expect her to play kiss up all the time helped, although the thought of arguing with him made her feel a little weak. Look at the way he'd taken over the couch, occupying not only his space but hers also. Just from that alone, she got a pretty clear idea of what he meant when he said *dominant*.

She wet her dry lips and regretted it immediately when his gaze dropped to her mouth. Somehow she could almost feel his lips on hers. His lips would be firm and—*Stay on task, Mac. Appear businesslike and maybe he'll act the same*. She could handle business interactions quite competently. She cleared her throat. "Ah. When does all this start? You'll need to give me an idea of what to wear ahead of time and when you expect me to be available." And just for sheer contrariness, since he'd said she didn't have to be under his thumb all the time, she pushed his hand away from her hair.

He didn't smile, although she could see laughter in his eyes, and she realized he'd won this round. If they were having a war, she'd just given him information, since he now knew his touch made her uncomfortable. "This isn't going to work, you know," she blurted out. "I don't like being touched. At all. Everyone will see that and know that we're not together."

Moving slightly closer, he tugged on her hair, then put his hand on her nape, and his touch felt more intimate than another man's kiss. Why? The heat from his palm penetrated her skin as his fingers closed just enough to remind her of his ruthless grip yesterday when he'd held her down and spanked her. The coffee in her cup rippled as her hand started to shake. She set the cup on her thigh to hide the telltale sign and looked up to meet his knowing gaze.

Not taking his hand from her neck, he leaned just an inch forward, invading her personal space. "Whether you enjoy being touched or not isn't what this is about. I require your submission and your honesty, nothing more."

His thumb rubbed up and down in the hollow under her ear. She hadn't realized how sensitive that patch of skin could be. Her tiny movement back made his grip tighten, and she got nowhere. Goose bumps broke out on her arms. "So you still want to do this? Me as your sub?"

"Yes, MacKensie. We will continue, and earlier than I had anticipated. I received a call this morning from Peter. A friend is having a party at the club tonight, and Cynthia, the woman I told you about, plans to attend."

"Tonight? You must be joking." Mac's orderly thoughts scattered into the corners of her mind. "But…but…I don't have clothes; I don't know what to do. I—"

"No problem. Do you have any interviews today?"

The thought of lying crossed her mind and disappeared under the slight narrowing of his eyes. "No. I set everything up for Monday."

"Excellent. Then today we'll go shopping."

"We?"

"Oh yes, pet. Definitely 'we.'"

✧ ✧ ✧ ✧ ✧

Later that day, Alex suppressed a grin as MacKensie wandered past latex corsets and leather bustiers, rubber miniskirts and thigh-high boots. And then he chose clothing for her to suit his preferences. She might as well start learning some of the various forms submission could entail. Lucky for her, he didn't enjoy twenty-four-hour mastery. Unlucky for her, he did occasionally enjoy dominance outside of the bedroom.

Like now.

"MacKensie."

She turned, and her eyes widened at the garments he held out to her.

"Put these on. I'll wait outside the door to see if they fit."

Her eyes narrowed, spine straightening until her height increased by almost an inch, which still left her half a foot shorter than he was. "I choose my own clothing, and I judge whether it fits."

"Not this time, pet." Alex kept his voice soft.

Not being at all slow, she caught the command. With a glare, she snatched the clothes and stalked into an empty fitting room.

She probably didn't realize the allure of a woman's ass when she's stomping. Or how arousing a sub's defiance could be to a dominant. And this one—he shook his head—could prove to be quite a trial to his control. He'd topped subs before and kept the interaction platonic; not everything had to be about sex, after all. But there was definitely a sexual component in the dynamics between him and MacKensie. She pulled at him—*strongly*—and he could see the same pull in her. But she didn't want to recognize that.

If she truly felt no attraction to him, he wouldn't think twice about observing her restrictions. But if fear corralled her sexuality? Then that was part of a Dom's mandate—to explore those fears. But only if he had her trust to do so.

So he needed to gauge the attraction, help her see that in herself, and earn her trust. Enjoying the thought of a challenge, he leaned against the door frame to wait.

When she appeared, he knew it had been worth the wait. An embarrassed flush highlighted her cheekbones almost as nicely as the French-maid's corset showcased her round breasts. The white lace and ribbon decorating the black latex gave her a fragile appearance, one that would be accentuated when she had on the garters and G-string that she held in her hand along with the other accessories.

"That will do nicely," he said.

"You cannot be serious." Her brown eyes sparked with indignation. "I'm not going to—"

When he lifted his eyebrows, she managed to cut off the rest of her protest.

"Wait in there," he said. "You'll need at least one more outfit."

She actually growled as she retreated.

"Surely Nordstroms doesn't have kinky clothing," MacKensie said. As they entered the fancy department store, she was all too aware of Alex's guiding hand on her lower back. He touched her—often—and always stood just a few inches too close. She knew he did it deliberately. Since he'd done nothing blatantly sexual that she could challenge him on, she tried to pretend his actions didn't unsettle her.

He bent down to murmur in her ear, his warm breath washing across her neck and making the hairs on her arms rise. "We're done with kink. Now we're shopping for formal wear for the party you want to attend."

"I want to attend? Does that mean you don't?" When she turned to look up at him, he was still so close that her lips grazed his cheek. She froze.

Rather than stepping away, he slowly straightened, his lips brushing against hers, as if accidentally. Only the crinkling of the lines at the corners of his eyes told her he'd done it deliberately. That, and the fact that every move he made was as controlled as the words he used.

"Normally I'd make a short appearance and leave." He touched her chin lightly with a finger. "But to do a good job of networking for you, we'll need to spend the evening."

He'd do that for her? An odd uneasiness lodged in the pit of her stomach, one having nothing to do with his teasing games. Jim and Mary had shown her a selfless generosity, but they'd thought of her as a daughter. Her sorority sisters in college had befriended her and given her etiquette lessons, thinking of her as a challenge. But men...men didn't help women. Not unless they wanted something, and Fontaine already had her under his thumb. He didn't need to do this.

Head tilted, he studied her face. "I've rarely seen that amount of disbelief when I ask a woman to a dance," he murmured. "But this isn't the place to discuss it." He guided her forward through the aisles of clothing.

If he thought she'd talk about her reaction or why, he was sadly mistaken. Not a chance.

A minute later, she planted her feet as something else occurred to her. "I didn't mind your paying for the...the kinky clothing since it's more for your problem than mine, but you can't buy me formal wear. That's not right."

He turned, his piercing blue eyes as focused as a laser from a science-fiction novel. Then he smiled and ran his hands up and down her arms, less a sexual than a comforting gesture. "MacKensie, I doubt you could afford what you need. It's my pleasure to get it for you."

She knew better. Gifts came first, followed by demands. She wasn't that kind of person anymore. "I can't accept, but thank you."

When she tried to step back, his hands tightened on her arms, holding her firmly in place. "I see. Well then, how about a trade? A lifetime of free care for Butler in exchange for my purchasing everything I think you'll need while you remain under my care."

"Under your care?"

"Yes, *pet*," he said, deliberately emphasizing the word. "I believe that is the bargain we made yesterday. This just adds a codicil to it."

"What are you, a lawyer?"

When he grinned, the sternness left his face. "I have a law degree, yes, but I'm mostly a boring businessman."

"You couldn't be boring if you tried," she muttered, then realized he still held her arms, apparently oblivious to the people having to detour around them. He'd probably wait there forever for his damned answer, wouldn't he? Considering the exorbitant price tags for the T-shirts on the rack beside them, the fancy clothing must be horrendously expensive. Even a lifetime of vet care might not cover it. But he obviously wasn't lacking for money, and he'd made an effort to salvage her pride. "All right. We have a deal."

"Good girl." He released her and headed toward the elevator.

Despite the fact that he wore jeans, he obviously exuded the scent of money, for the saleswoman in the formal-wear department upstairs pounced on him like a cat discovering a mouse. With an effort, Mac concealed the fact she was shaking in her sneakers and tried to emulate his polite reserve.

Arm around Mac, Alex instructed the woman about what he had in mind, consulting Mac only to get her shoe size. Mac couldn't decide if she felt insulted or coddled. Coddled won out since she had no clue how to buy a formal gown; she'd never bought one in her life. Her college finances sure hadn't extended that far. She'd only been in the sorority because of the influence and funds provided by an alumnus friend of Mary's.

The saleswoman returned with an armload of gowns that she held up for Alex's approval. Not Mac's.

"If you like them so much, maybe you should try them on," Mac muttered.

Alex laughed and then shocked her stupid by kissing the top of her head.

She pulled on gown after gown, with the saleswoman helping her lace and tie and button and zip. Gold, blue, black. With each one, Alex made noncommittal noises. The final hanger held a long, full-skirted gown in pink, and Mac sneered at it. *The color of cheerleaders.* "I never wear pink."

"Pink would be lovely on you," the saleswoman said. "Your man has a good eye for color." She whisked the gown over Mac's head.

Mac had barely a glimpse before the woman pushed her gently out of the room to where Alex waited on a plush couch. Legs outstretched, one arm resting along the back, he looked thoroughly at home. His eyebrows rose when he saw her this time. "That's lovely on you, MacKensie."

As warmth bloomed inside her, she tried not to reveal how much the compliment meant.

He twirled a finger in the air, a silent command to turn.

She did and—to hell with it—enjoyed the feel of the luxurious fabric swirling around her bare legs. She caught a glimpse of herself in the mirrors and stopped dead. *Whoa, look at that, Miss Elegance.* She turned one way, then the other, admiring herself, before remembering who watched.

"But pink?" she said, making a token protest.

"Pink looks good on you," he said mildly. "We'll take this one," he told the saleslady. "Please select the appropriate undergarments, hose, and shoes." He tapped his fingers on the arm of the couch, thinking. "A purse and a cape also. The evening will be chilly."

Mac's mouth dropped open. As the saleslady scurried away, beaming like a woman whose commission had just gone through the roof, Mac realized she should have put a limit on how much Fontaine could spend. "That's too much." Maybe most women would gloat over the windfall, but it made her feel obligated.

"We have a deal." Alex rose to stand beside her. With a faint smile, he ran a finger down her cheek, his touch somehow more intimate that any john who'd pounded into her.

Chapter Five

S he changed the bandage on his back when they got home. Only a tiny bit of clear pink drainage had stained the gauze, and the wound was healing nicely. As she taped the gauze down, she couldn't help but notice the long lines of his torso and the contoured muscles of his back. Under her fingers, his warm skin felt velvety soft over disconcertingly hard muscles beneath. No businessman she'd ever seen had muscles like that.

Bemused, she looked up and met his penetrating gaze in the mirror. *Oops.* She stepped back hurriedly, only to have him grasp her wrist.

"MacKensie, it's time we talked." Still holding her wrist, not her hand, he led her to the family room and pointed to the couch. "Sit there."

As she took a seat, he opened the curtains to display a magnificent view of the Sound, with the white-capped Olympics beyond, then disappeared into the kitchen.

Mac leaned her head on her hand and studied the mountains. Yeah, they really were gorgeous. Yet right now she wanted cozy instead. A place deep inside her ached with the need to be rocking on her porch swing with the neighbor's cat a warm weight in her lap. Red and orange leaves would be swirling down from the big maple, and she would grumble to Fluffball about having to rake them all up.

Before she could descend into a major homesickness attack, Butler got up from the rug by the fireplace and leaned against her leg with a heavy sigh, as if he'd worked a twelve-hour day. She leaned forward to pet him and whispered in his ear, "I had a rough day too, baby."

Alex returned and handed her a glass of dark red wine.

After taking it, she regarded him warily. "What are we going to talk about?"

He sat down in the middle of the couch. Why did the man always crowd into her space?

"In a couple of hours, we're going to my club to spend the evening," he said. "A friend and his sub had a private collaring ceremony earlier today, and they plan to celebrate at Chains. You'll be on display as my sub, MacKensie."

Good thing he'd given her the wine. She took a hefty gulp. Good stuff. Smoother than any she'd tasted before. "And what exactly will that display entail?"

One corner of his mouth turned up. "Your first lesson is this: what we do—what *you* do—is entirely up to *me*."

Oh now, didn't that just sound great? Undoubtedly, protest would be futile. She was being assimilated and liked it no more than Captain Picard had.

He sipped his wine, studying her until she felt like a lab mouse. "Let's talk about diseases. Have you been tested since the last time you had sex?"

"I've been tested." Jim had insisted on it after taking her in. "I'm clean." *But hadn't Alex promised no sex?* "But—"

"Any chance you're pregnant?"

God forbid. "No. I have an IUD." *Thanks to Ajax, who didn't want to have any of his "girls" sidelined with pregnancies if and when a condom broke.* She'd replaced the IUD in college when she'd started dating and hoping… Well, she'd been more optimistic back then.

"Any medical problems? Any at all, MacKensie?" he warned. "I don't like surprises."

"No. I don't have any medical problems."

"Have you ever been tied up or restrained in any way?" he asked. "Are you claustrophobic?"

She choked on her wine. "Um. No, and maybe a little." *Just don't shut me up behind a locked door.* "I don't like small, dark places."

"Good to know. Have you ever been whipped? Beaten? Flogged? Hit at all?"

To each question, she shook her head.

"Spanked?"

No one has ever cared enough to spank me. She swallowed. "Only by you." When his eyes narrowed, moving from her fingers clenching the wineglass to her eyes, she had to look away.

A finger under her chin forced her gaze back to his. "When was the last time you made love with anyone?"

She shoved his hand away and snapped, "I've never 'made love' with anyone."

"All right," he said easily. "When was the last time you had sex?"

"About twelve years ago." And when that john had complained about her unenthusiastic blowjob, Ajax had decided she needed incentive. After the two men left, she'd crawled out of the alley to collapse at Jim's feet.

"That's a long time, little cat." Alex's low voice broke into her thoughts. He tucked a strand of hair behind her ear and then massaged her shoulder. "What happened? You would have been...sixteen?"

How did he know that? Oh right. The application she'd filled out for Exchanges had her birth date. "Nothing happened."

"Don't lie to me, pet."

"Well then." She tried to ignore the warmth of the hand on her shoulder. "It's none of your business."

"Actually it is. As your Dom, I need your history so I know what land mines to avoid. Or head for."

Head for? But she could see why a person into kinky stuff might worry about emotional hang-ups. "I had some—a—bad experience with sex. That's all," she said stiffly.

"Has anyone tried to give you a good experience since then?"

"No point." His finger slid under the collar of her shirt to stroke the juncture of her neck and shoulder. How did he find such sensitive places on her body? "I'm not interested in sex. At all."

"I see." His eyes crinkled. "And what would happen if you inadvertently became interested? Aroused?"

"I-I…" She glared at him. "It won't happen, so there's no—"

"In that case, I have your permission to take the next step? To change our play to sexual?"

Did he not understand the "won't happen" phrase she'd used? "Listen, I don't want you deluding yourself that I'm interested in sex when I'm not."

"Ah. So you require objective proof that we both can see. I understand the need." He tilted his head. "So if your nipples become erect in a warm room, and your pussy gets wet enough on the outside to dampen my hand, is that a sign of arousal?"

She flushed at just the thought of his hand…there. Damned lawyer. She crossed her arms over her chest. If her nipples had peaked, she *so* didn't want to know. "No."

"MacKensie, I should warn you that lying is punished."

The thought of being spanked again sent a tiny shiver through her.

The corner of his mouth turned up for a second before his eyes chilled. "Now give me the truth."

"Yes, all right. Wet means aroused, okay?"

"And if you're aroused, then, as your Dom, I will determine how sexual in nature our play becomes. If you become unaroused, I stop. Have we an agreement?"

"I'd rather leave it with no sex at all."

"I'm not comfortable with those limitations," he said softly. "As your Dom, I give you what you need, not necessarily what you want."

✧ ✧ ✧ ✧ ✧

Alex kept his hand on his sub's bare arm as they entered Chains. Because of Lynn and Bob's party, the private BDSM club was busier than normal, with every station in use. Whips *snapped* and floggers *splatted*, accompanied by moans and screams and whimpers. Most of the rising and falling hum of conversations came from the crowded bar area. The music of Nine Inch Nails' "Meet Your Master" blasted down from the dance floor upstairs, where people lined the rails, watching the scenes downstairs. Upstairs on the left, the quieter safe-lounge area held more people.

"Kink is a popular sport these days, isn't it?" MacKensie murmured, looking around with wide eyes.

"It is." Grasping her arms, he held her out in front of him, taking a second to appreciate the view. The dark leather bustier not only matched her eyes but also emphasized her tiny waist and pushed her breasts up in a way that tempted fingers to explore. The bloodred latex skirt stretched over her firm, round ass, stopping just below her cheeks. He'd considered letting her wear heels but decided she needed a constant reminder of her submission, so she was both bare legged and barefoot.

His decree of no underwear had received a horrified look, then a stubborn one, and finally compliance. Very reluctant compliance. This would be an interesting night with her denial of her submissive nature and his need to dominate.

"Why are you staring at me?" she asked, scowling at him.

Definitely interesting. He tightened his grip to remind her of his strength and ability to hold her in place all night if needed. "MacKensie, do you recall our agreement?"

Her eyes dropped.

"That's better." He'd held off on swamping her with all the protocols, but this would be a good time for some more. "Now some rules: In a club or anytime we're in Dom/sub roles, you stay silent unless spoken to. You address any Dom as 'Sir' and any Domme as 'Ma'am.' If you need to ask for something, you say, 'Sir, may I have permission to speak, Sir?'"

"You have got to be kidding. That's—" She halted at his frown.

"Making a mistake can and will get you disciplined, little cat." At his words, a tremor rippled through her. *Punishment, discipline*, and *spanking* were trigger words for her, and the haunted look in her eyes indicated an emotional response rather than an erotic one. Another area to explore. Soon.

He continued. "I prefer that you keep your eyes on me; I like to see what's in them." He ran his hands up and down her arms, feeling the soft, soft skin and the toned muscles hidden beneath a woman's gentle padding. "Keep your eyes down with other dominants. Some take offense at a sub meeting their gaze."

Her hands tightened into fists. But even in the dim light of the room, he could see a slight flush of excitement appear on her cheekbones. He eyed the bustier that hid her nipples. Maybe he should have forced her to wear only a skirt. Then again, the leather laces could be easily undone. "Is there any part of this that you don't understand?"

She shook her head.

"Your answer should be 'no, Sir.'"

"No, Sir."

"Very nice." He let approval warm his voice. The way she drank it in like a thirsty kitten made him want to wrap her in his arms.

"Alex, you made it!" Bob pushed through the crowd, trailed by his sub.

"How could I not come to celebrate with you?" Alex shook Bob's hand. "Congratulations. You're a lucky man."

"I know." Bob put his arm around Lynn, pulling her forward. "Oh I know."

The slim brunette leaned into her Dom, her eyes glowing. Every few seconds, she fingered the thin collar around her neck, stroking the leather as if she wore the finest of diamond jewelry.

Alex glanced at Bob for permission and received a nod before kissing Lynn's cheek. "Felicitations, sweetheart."

She beamed at him.

Bob looked at MacKensie and raised his eyebrows. "Well. I heard you and Cynthia had parted ways, but she called it a false rumor."

"No rumor." Alex smothered his irritation before putting an arm around his little vet and pulling her closer. "I'm working with MacKensie at the moment. She's very new to the scene, and this is her first time out openly as a sub."

Mac kept her eyes on the ground, but she could actually feel the appraising look from Alex's friend.

"Very pretty." Bob snorted. "Cynthia's reaction should be interesting."

Lynn giggled.

"Doubtful," Alex said in a cold voice.

When his arm around Mac tightened, she didn't resist, needing the feeling of being protected more than she needed to avoid contact. The atmosphere seemed more intense than the public BDSM clubs she'd visited. She'd expected to see subs getting flogged, caned, even sights like the person having hot wax being tipped onto her stomach from a candle. But here, the observers were more focused, and the people negotiating a scene were more serious. In fact, one Dom had actually taken out a list on a piece of paper to go over it, point by point, with a thin male sub. That Dom looked up just then and met Mac's eyes.

She dropped her gaze immediately. *Oops.* This not looking at Doms wasn't an easy rule to remember.

"We've commandeered an area near the far end, between the stockade and the St. Andrew's cross. C'mon over," Bob said.

Still within the curve of Alex's arm, Mac walked through the room. By a massive wooden St. Andrew's cross, Bob's group occupied a sitting area of leather couches and chairs. As Alex received a chorus of hellos and welcomes, Mac unobtrusively checked out his friends. The mostly male Doms wore either leathers or black clothing, much like the black slacks and black silk shirt Alex had on. Their ages ranged from thirties to fifties, and most were fairly good-looking, with a couple of men almost as gorgeous as Alex. One female Domme had a male sub, another a female.

As Alex took a chair, Mac looked for one too, then noticed every sub was kneeling on the floor. She didn't want to embarrass Alex, so she did the same, trying not to flash everyone and cursing her short skirt and lack of underwear. Once situated, she checked her posture against the other subs—kneeling, hands palms up on knees, back straight—then glanced up at Alex.

His eyes and smile showed his pleasure even before he leaned forward and stroked her hair. "Very observant, little cat. You look lovely."

The compliment in his deep voice seemed to glide right through her skin and into her insides, creating a warm glow that lessened her insecurity. Not that the glow lasted as comments from the other Doms came hard and fast. She forced her gaze to stay on the floor.

"New sub?"

"Pretty little thing."

"Looks a little feisty; 'bout time you had a challenge."

His hand rested on her shoulder possessively. "Her name is MacKensie, and she's new to the scene."

When their attention turned elsewhere, she gave a sigh of relief—one that was too noticeable, she understood, when Alex gave a quiet laugh and squeezed her shoulder.

His touch felt good. Too good. He watched her closely and touched her too easily. A slight tremor ran through her, and she edged away from him. He glanced down at her, focused on her a minute, then removed his hand.

And then she felt lonely. *Frak*.

As the subs stayed silent, the Doms discussed plans for the following week and upcoming events. When no waitress appeared, they designated two subs to fetch drinks. Then two of the Doms asked for Alex's opinion on a scene across the room, some sort of knife stuff that sounded appallingly bloody.

"All right," Alex told them, then looked down at her. "MacKensie, do you want to see this?"

"I get to choose?" Wasn't he supposed to make all the decisions?

He smiled, his hand cupping her cheek. "I know you don't mind blood, but I don't know how you feel about one person deliberately cutting another."

She shuddered. That didn't sound at all pleasant.

"And there's my answer." Alex rose. "Remain here. I'll be back in a few minutes."

Not a problem. Just after he walked away, she realized she'd missed her chance to ask a vital question: where was the restroom? Her bladder felt like an overinflated balloon, and the tight skirt made it worse. She looked around. Two Doms, one Domme, and a handful of subs remained. The other subs wore clothing much like hers, although one was completely naked. Another wore only jeweled clamps on her nipples—*ouch*—with a chain running between them, and a very skimpy thong.

Mac shook her head in wonder. Apparently she'd gotten off lightly when Alex had chosen her outfit.

Clothing or not, she still had to pee. When a gorgeous brunette kneeling beside the adjacent chair looked over, Mac asked, "Are we allowed to go to the bathroom? I'm dying here."

Expressionless, the brunette eyed Mac. Then she smiled slightly and pointed. "The restrooms are across the room. You should be able to get there and back before the Doms return."

"Thanks." After pushing to her feet, Mac hurried across the room, past two flogging scenes and one man touching some electrical thing to intimate places on his male sub. Looked painful as all get-out.

Once she'd used the toilet and managed to wiggle her skirt back into place, she retraced her steps, using the St. Andrew's cross as her heading.

Halfway there, a hefty Dom in battered leathers stopped her. "Brown top, red skirt, medium height, yellow-brown hair. You must be MacKensie."

Mac blinked. "Um. Yes."

"Good enough. I got your safe word and conditions." He snapped a metal handcuff on her, whipped her around, and put one on the other wrist, just like in a cop show. And just like a show, he pushed her forward.

"Hey, let go!" Mac tried to jerk away, but he had a good grip on her and must have outweighed her by a good hundred pounds. She raised her voice. "I don't know you. Let go of me." She kicked out at him without managing to hit anything vital, and suddenly the hand clamped around her arm felt like Arlene's. *Dragging her to the closet. Helpless.* Her hands chilled. "No no no!"

He cut off her screams by stuffing a rubber ball into her mouth, securing the elastic band behind her head. With her hands restrained, she couldn't fight, couldn't get it off.

"C'mon, little bitch. Time for punishment." Letting go of her, he shoved her ahead of him toward a scene area that held a stockade-like thing.

Horror ran through her at the sight of the single hole in the board. Not designed to restrain a person's hands, but their neck. A short whip lay on the floor beside it. *No no no.* Whirling, she kicked out at the man and nailed his thigh.

He yelled and grabbed her arm, one huge hand raised. Turning her face away, she braced herself for the blow. For the pain.

Chapter Six

I t never came.

"I believe we have a problem here." Alex's voice. He had caught the man's wrist, held it frozen in the air.

Relief swirled through Mac so fast, her head spun. She tried to tug away.

The man gripped her arm tighter. "No problem, dude, except your interfering in my scene." Her assailant yanked her out of Alex's reach.

"It may be your scene," Alex said. "But that is my sub."

"Hey, man, she came to me." The bastard had the nerve to shake her shoulder as if to prove his point.

Mac shook her head frantically, tried to speak through the gag.

"She doesn't appear to agree."

"Just part of the scene. She wanted a rape scene, set it up special. I didn't hear her using her safe word either."

Alex's eyes on her were cold. Furious.

He believed the man. *Oh please, no.* She shook her head again, her eyes filling with tears. He'd leave her here, let her be hurt, and—

"Remove her gag," Alex said. He glanced at an old man standing nearby, watching the show. "Find a dungeon monitor."

"On his way already," the old man said.

"Now listen, asshole—" The cruel-faced man dragged her farther from Alex.

"Gentlemen, what seems to be the problem?" Another man wearing a bright orange vest over a black shirt frowned at the men.

"This little bitch set up a rape scene with me, and now this asshole says she's his sub and butted into my scene."

The dungeon monitor raised his eyebrows. "Considering Alex is one of the founding members of this club, I have trouble believing that." He jerked a chin at Mac. "Let's hear from the sub. Remove the cuffs and the gag."

The bastard unlocked her cuffs. When he let her go to pocket them, Mac shoved him as hard as she could and ran straight for Alex. His arms closed around her, holding her to him. After a breath, she pulled the gag off and turned far enough to throw it at the man, then tried to burrow into Alex even farther. His scent of subtle, rich cologne and soap surrounded her, and his firm embrace held her against his solid body. She'd found her shelter.

He pressed a kiss to the top of her head. "Let's have a seat and discuss this," he said.

She stiffened, cold fear rising inside her. Clutching his arms, she stared up into his forbidding face. "Don't let him take me. Please, Alex, don't." Now that she was free, an uncontrollable shaking started deep inside her. *The feel of a fist hitting her jaw, the shock of being slapped, pain from… No. No memories. Not now.* Her tears spilled over, and an ugly sobbing noise escaped. She put her hands over her mouth.

"Shhh, sweetheart." Alex scooped her up in his arms and cuddled her to his chest as if she were a puppy. "No one is taking you anywhere. But I need to know what happened."

She buried her face against his shoulder, unable to stop the violent shudders racking her body. A minute later he sat down on a couch, but he kept her in his lap, one arm fixed around her waist, one hand stroking her back. Her cheek rested against him, and she heard the slow thud of his heart, felt the easy rise and fall of his chest.

He wasn't worried. He could take care of this. Of her.

Footsteps. Then the dungeon monitor said, "Alex, this is Steel, and Steel says the sub's name is MacKensie. He asked her if that was her name."

"Asked?" Alex questioned. "Why did you need to ask her name?"

"I wanted to make sure I had the right sub, and she was. Brown top, red skirt, yellow-brown hair, name of MacKensie."

Alex's body tightened, and anger turned his voice to ice. "Then MacKensie didn't set this up with you. Someone else did."

"Well, yeah. She wanted a stranger to grab her and whip her. That was the scenario. Wouldn't work if she knew me, now would it?"

Clutching Alex's shirt like a security blanket, Mac lifted her head to look at Steel. He had a perplexed look on his face as he ran his hand through shaggy hair.

The dungeon monitor scowled. "I'm getting a really bad feeling about this." He looked at her, started to speak, and then frowned at Alex instead. "Permission to speak to your sub?"

"Of course."

"Did you ask someone to set this up, MacKensie?"

She shook her head, her throat so tense, no words could escape.

"Well, fuck, look at her shake," Steel muttered. "Are you telling me I grabbed the wrong person?"

"No," Alex said softly. "I think this was a setup. Just not the one you'd planned." He turned Mac in his arms until she faced him. When she tried to bury her head, he used a finger to raise her chin. "We need you to talk to us, little cat." His eyes pinned her gaze to his. "I left you kneeling beside the chair. Why did you leave?"

She tried to swallow, but the spit stuck in her throat. Her grip tightened on his shirt, and she breathed in, trying to find the calm place inside herself, the one where she used to hide. Another breath. "I-I had to…bathroom."

His lips curved, and his voice softened. "I have a bad habit of forgetting you women piss three times as often as men. So you went to the bathroom. Alone?"

"I thought I could get back before you returned."

"How did you know where the bathroom is?"

"The other sub told me."

"Describe her to me, MacKensie." Alex's eyes had turned the color of polar ice.

"Brunette. Beautiful." Mac closed her eyes, trying to remember. "Tall. She looks like a model. A dark red corset thing."

"That who you talked with?" the dungeon monitor asked Steel.

"Nah. I'd remember someone like that." Steel pulled out a piece of paper and handed it to the monitor. "A barmaid gave me this. It spells it all out. Even safe words and gestures. She didn't use either."

The monitor glanced at Mac. "What's your safe word?"

Safe word? She looked up at Alex and whispered, "What's a safe word?"

"Fuck me," Steel exploded. "How the hell can she not—"

"She's so new to the scene that she should be glowing green," Alex said. "We haven't even done anything that would require a safe word."

A noise came from Steel, a grating sound as his teeth clenched. "Did she—Did you—Hell. Permission to speak to your sub?"

Alex snorted. "Granted."

When Steel leaned forward, Mac couldn't help but cringe back, her bare feet scrambling uselessly on the couch. Alex's arms tightened, trapping her on his lap.

Steel winced, and his face turned to concrete. "You didn't want this at all, did you?"

Mac shook her head as the shaking started again. She shoved her face in the hollow of Alex's shoulder.

"Girl, look at me."

Silence. The men waited. For her.

Okay, Mac, show a few guts. Suck it up and handle it. Her fingers ached from her grip on Alex's shirt, but she managed to turn.

To her surprise, Steel looked more tired than terrifying as he said, "A safe word is a word not usually used in everyday talk, and if a sub uses it, everything stops. A gesture is used if the sub is gagged. If you'd used either, I'd have stopped. Right then." He rubbed his hands over his face. "Fuck. Since you didn't know about them, you wouldn't use them. I'm sorry, girl."

He fished a card out of his pocket and handed it to the monitor. "If you catch the asshole who did this, I'll be pleased to do anything needed to take him down. Very pleased." He handed one to Alex. "If there's anything I can do to help her or you, call me."

Catch the asshole? Coldness ran up Mac's spine as everything began to make sense. Someone had set her up to be whipped. Why?

"You got any idea of who did this, Alex?" the monitor asked.

"Oh yes. The trouble is, there's no proof," Alex growled. "But I know. A sub wants me—obsession-type-want."

The dungeon monitor frowned. "You were with Cynthia last time I saw you here. The society girl."

Alex nodded.

"Hell." The dungeon monitor glanced at the paper. "Drake's going to blow his stack when he hears about this. But he'll investigate up one side and down another. If the barmaid remembers anything… But they're so busy tonight, I'm not holding out much hope."

"Do what you can. I'll do the same."

Alex could barely control his rage as he carried MacKensie back to the group. He considered leaving immediately, but letting her flee the club would reinforce her fears, legitimate as they were. And she needed to face the real assailant.

Dammit. Although Cynthia should be arrested, no BDSM club welcomed publicity, and few members would volunteer to testify.

Alex settled in a chair, pulling Mac closer to him. He'd never felt such satisfaction as when she had hurtled herself into his arms, knowing he'd protect her.

Her shivering had disappeared once Steel left. Tough little sub—his jaw tensed—who had been hurt because of him.

"Sir?" One of the subs approached warily, her eyes wide.

Alex took a breath to smother the anger and gave her a smile.

The sub relaxed. "Sir, I have drinks for you and your sub."

"Thank you." Alex nodded to the table beside the arm of the chair. "Right there, please."

The sub obeyed and trotted away. Alex handed Mac the gin and tonic he'd ordered earlier for her and picked up his scotch.

She sipped, blinked, and sipped again. "I haven't had one of these since college," she said and actually smiled. Two more sips and she looked at him full in the face. "Thanks for the rescue. And for believing me."

He nodded. Such big brown eyes. To see them filled with terror and tears had seared his heart. A ball of anger still burned deep inside him, one with no place to go.

"What are you going to do about her?" she asked quietly. She glanced at Cynthia, who knelt at Brian's feet two chairs down.

"If a witness turns up, we'll look at prosecution. I'm going to talk with the management here and at the other clubs. And with the Doms. She'll discover the BDSM world is smaller than she knows and a lot more unfriendly." He stroked MacKensie's golden hair. "I'm sorry, MacKensie. Our lifestyle has many safeguards, but none that could prevent this kind of end run around them."

"Yeah, I can see that." She leaned her head against him. The gesture, now, when she wasn't terrified, showed her trust in him had grown.

"Sir, permission to speak?"

Alex looked up at the sound of the smooth, rich voice. Cynthia knelt at his feet, eyes downcast. He knew she wouldn't incriminate herself; she was a very smart woman. But he'd see what she had to say. "Speak."

"Master Bob said you've taken that sub on for training, but I can see that you are not intimate with her. I would be pleased to serve the needs that she can't." Cynthia opened her corset, letting her full breasts spill out. Tall and slender and with those augmented breasts, Cynthia was a walking wet dream. And in his case, a walking nightmare.

Alex suppressed a growl. "I don't—"

Giving a tiny duplication of his growl, Mac glared at Cynthia. "He doesn't need you, you overbred cow; he has me." And she grabbed his hand and shoved it between her legs.

Chapter Seven

"Well, now," Alex murmured in a low rumble that sent nerves racing up Mac's arms.

Oh frak, what have I done? Mac froze, shocked at her own behavior.

Alex's lips curved, and then he gave Cynthia a dismissive look. "I'm more than adequately served. Leave."

The sub jerked back as if Alex had slapped her. Mac almost laughed as Cynthia stalked away, rehooking her corset, heading toward the front of the club. Apparently the Dom she'd accompanied had left. Smart man.

Suddenly Alex's hand pressed against Mac's pussy. She jumped, her gaze shooting to his amused eyes. His hand felt huge between her thighs, and hot against her bare labia.

"If you keep rearranging our bargain," he said, "I might not be able to keep up."

"I…" Trapped by his blue gaze, she couldn't find the right words to say. *I didn't want you to take her? I was jealous? I wanted to be mean?* All of them were true. "But…"

His eyes crinkled. "You, little cat, do not have permission to speak." He lifted his hand from the juncture between her legs. "And you're not ready to be played with down here…yet." His fingers threaded through her hair, and he leaned forward, tipping her back against the arm of the chair. Her gasp opened her lips, but he didn't shove his tongue down her throat, didn't grab her breast.

Why hadn't he groped her down there? She'd sure given him the chance.

Instead his tongue traced over her lower lip in a teasing slide. Then the upper. His mouth brushed against her cheek, her chin, her neck; his lips were firm yet smooth. Not wet or sloppy at all.

When he returned to her mouth, he nibbled her lower lip, then sucked on it lightly. Slanting his mouth across hers, he kissed her, his tongue only caressing her lips, no further. He moved down her neck with tiny nips and licks and kisses. She shivered when he bit the muscle at the top of her shoulder, holding it between his teeth long enough to send goose bumps down her arms. Back up, ever so slowly, and this time when he took her lips, she opened to him, letting her tongue fence with his.

Never sloppy. He was even so careful that she wanted to push him a little. Her tongue slid into his mouth, and suddenly his hand fisted in her hair, holding her in place as he ravaged her mouth, the controlled violence shocking.

Exciting.

When he pulled back and licked over her lips, she took a deep breath. The air felt as if the temperature in the building had been raised too high. Then coolness wafted over her chest. She stiffened, looking down. Her bustier lay open, lacing undone, her breasts exposed.

Alex's arm felt like iron under her back, and that hand still held her hair. Held her trapped. Without taking his eyes from hers, he curved a big hand around her breast, his fingers hot against her skin. She inhaled sharply at the unexpectedly erotic sensations shooting through her as he caressed her. The surge of…of something inside her frightened her, and she grasped his wrist and ripped her gaze from his.

"Look at me, MacKensie," he said, voice deepening. When her eyes returned to his, he smiled slightly. "Good girl. Now let go of me, or I'll restrain you."

"You wouldn't."

But his eyes didn't waver.

He would. She forced her fingers to release his wrist. "You promised. I'm not aroused," she whispered. Fear curled inside her to join with the unsettling tension, and an odd temptation to let him continue, to have his hands…everywhere.

"You told Cynthia you'd take care of me," he whispered back. "Can you tolerate another ten minutes of being fondled?"

She'd been an idiot to offer herself instead of Cynthia, but he hadn't asked her to do that. Her big mouth had run amok all by itself. Okay, ten minutes… What was another person groping her anyway? At least she *liked* him as opposed to the others. She managed a short nod.

When the sun lines at the corners of his eyes crinkled, and his eyes heated, a trickle of worry crept into her. What could he do in ten minutes with just his hands?

She found out exactly what he could do when his hand on her breast moved, and his fingers circled one nipple, then the other, grazing over the bumpy areolae to the jutting peaks. Peaks—her nipples were hard, and the room wasn't cold. Surely she couldn't be aroused.

His index finger circled one nub, around and around, until that nipple actually ached. He did the other, and the feeling was… His fingers closed on one rigid peak, rolling it gently, then giving it a small pinch that sent a stab of excitement through her body and seemed to awaken nerves in her pussy. A throbbing in her groin joined the throbbing in her nipples.

She swallowed a moan as he alternated between her breasts, back and forth, pressing the nipples hard, then harder, until each controlled pinch hurt and yet increased the burning hunger inside her. A moan escaped her.

Satisfaction glimmered in his eyes before he tightened the arm under her back, bringing her breasts up to his mouth. His lips closed on one swollen nipple, and she found out just what hot and wet really meant. His tongue swirled around the peak, and suddenly she could almost feel it swirling on her clit; and then he sucked, a gentle pull, then more forcefully. The other breast the same. And back, this time sucking, and suddenly, a slow, careful bite on the peak.

"Ahhhh!" Her fingers dug into his shoulders in shock as electrifying sparks shot through her. Had that sound come from her? She pushed against his chest, horrified. She never lost control like that; she was a—Oh God, she wasn't a whore. Not anymore. Shame washed through her, filling her until there remained no room for arousal.

He'd drawn back when she stiffened. His sharp eyes considered her face, then her hands and her breasts. "Why does being aroused scare you?" he asked softly.

She closed her eyes.

"No, look at me, little cat."

She could feel his intense gaze on her, like warmth stroking over her face; she could feel how he waited for her compliance. Her hands in fists, she opened her eyes.

"Good girl." His lips curved up in approval. "You told me you don't get aroused because of something in your past."

He waited for her nod.

"Why did that something make you frightened of your own response?"

Because whores don't feel. Because johns don't care. Men paid for an available body, not a responsive one. Because losing track of surroundings was a way to get hurt. "I just don't like it."

His eyes crinkled even as he shook his head. "You do like it, little cat. But you don't want to, because it scares you. There is a difference." His warm hand stroked over her breast again, and she was horrified to feel her nipple pucker and poke into his palm. "What would happen if you didn't have any choice? If you couldn't push my hands away or keep me from continuing? You could only feel."

The thought shut off her breathing for a second. Not have any control? Fear filled her even as heat seared through her veins, and her nipples tightened until they actually hurt.

He nodded as if she'd spoken. "Want and fear both. So how brave are you, little cat? Will you let me take you further?"

Her body urged for more. Her head said no, but she knew damned well that her head was screwed up. How brave was she? She didn't think her body would ever, ever be interested in sex again. Shouldn't she see…? *But what if I panic? What if I don't?* "All right," she whispered.

God, how could that approving smile of his make her feel so good inside?

He stroked her cheek. "Brave little cat. Trust isn't easy for you, is it? Because you don't fully trust me, we'll stay here in public. The club safe word is 'red.' Do you understand what it's for?"

"Yes, but—"

"Yes, what?" He frowned at her, recalling her to his rules.

"Yes, Sir."

"Good." He rose to his feet with her still in his arms.

"Hey!" She wiggled. What was he going to do?

"You don't have permission to speak, little cat. You may use your safe word if you need to." He walked across the room to a leather-covered table and laid her on it, then whipped a strap over her ribs to hold her in place. She'd thought he meant to control her by using his hands to hold her. Like he had been.

She struggled to sit up, and he pressed her shoulders down. "MacKensie. We have a deal. If you became aroused, I could continue, right?"

Heart pounding, she sucked in air as she stared up at him. His hands were warm on her shoulders, his eyes level. Patient. She had agreed. She gave him a short nod.

"And you agreed to submit to me, knowing what BDSM involved. You also agreed to continue a minute ago. Right?"

Oh God, she had agreed. Okay, okay. This was just part of BDSM, and he wasn't paying her. *I'm not a whore, just someone doing kinky things.* Kind of. She nodded again.

"Good." He smiled slightly, cupping her cheek, then touched her lips lightly with his. "I'm going to restrain you, little cat, because your mind, for whatever reason, thinks you shouldn't do this and tells you to stop. But I'm not going to stop, and there will be nothing you can do about it."

Even as he spoke, he pulled leather straps over her arms, her wrists. Then one across her hips over her skirt. To her shock, he flipped her skirt up and wrapped a Velcro cuff around her lower thigh. Bending her knee, he pushed her leg toward her shoulder and clipped the thigh cuff right beside her wrist. He did the same on the other side, and she lay on the table splayed open like a frog about to be cut up.

What was sexy about that? Yet the feeling of having her most intimate parts bared and vulnerable sent a shiver through her. She could see a few people around the edge of the scene area, watching.

Alex chuckled and rubbed his knuckles over her cheek, pulling her attention back to him. "Take a breath, sweetheart."

She pulled in a deep breath.

His eyes were very blue and seemed to fill her whole vision. "Good." He kissed her again, gently, lightly, coaxing her to respond. When she did, he pulled back, then ran his hands up and down her torso to the tender undersides of her breasts. To the nipples that had again started to pucker. When he sucked on the nipples, the tightness turned into a tingling ache of need.

Then she heard someone in the crowd laugh, turned her head, and saw their faces. She stiffened and made a useless attempt to move.

Alex lifted his head and studied her for a second. "Little cat, do you trust me not to leave you? Not for a second?"

Why was he asking her that? But he didn't say more. She bit her lip. Would he stay with her? Well, he'd saved her from that man and then held her. He hadn't abandoned her. She'd seen that he had his own code of honor. "Yes, Sir," she said.

"Ah." He smiled at her. "I like the trust I see growing. Now, I promise I won't hurt you while you're restrained here on the table. Do you trust me to keep my word?"

A whore learned to read people well. She usually knew when someone lied to her. He wasn't lying. "Yes, Sir." She swallowed. "What are you going to do?"

"I'm going to take a little more control from you, MacKensie. I will ask you to keep your eyes closed." From under the table, he lifted headphones. "You won't be able to see or hear, just to feel my hands on your body. My mouth on your pussy."

Her breath hitched at the image.

"You have your safe word, little cat. Now close your eyes." She did. When the earphones covered her ears, she heard the rhythmic sounds of the ocean: a low roar, then hissing. All she could hear was the ocean; all she could see was black. Had he left her? Her eyes popped open, and she looked right up into Alex's amused face. Like he knew she'd panic.

She caught a breath of Alex's rich aftershave just before his hand cupped her cheek, and he kissed her, gently, coaxing the response he knew she could give. After a minute, he lifted his head and touched her temple in an unspoken command.

Dammit, she wanted to be able to see.

He waited.

After giving him a glare that made his lips quirk, she closed her eyes.

His mouth covered hers again. As he toyed with her lips, nibbled on them, her anxiety diminished. And after a minute, many minutes, he moved. She had a second of panic. Then his hands touched her breasts, the feel of his slightly rough fingers already familiar. His lips closed around one nipple, his tongue hot against the sensitive tip as he sucked.

His mouth withdrew. Coolness over the wet nub, then…a pinching sensation. Not his fingers. The compression tightened right to the edge of pain and didn't loosen. *A clamp*. Like that other sub had worn. The steady pressure created a sizzling river of sensation between her breast and her groin. His hot mouth sucked on the other nipple, then the pressure again. The ache in her pussy increased.

His hand stroked down her stomach, trailing across the top of her skirt, then past and over her bare leg. He'd moved to the foot of the table, she realized, as his hands massaged her hips. When he stroked the exposed undersides of her thighs, it brought home how high and wide he'd parted her knees, leaving her open.

She tried to move her legs, and none of the straps gave, and the ocean rolled through the darkness as his hands moved closer to where she ached.

His hand pressed against her pussy for a second before stroking her thigh, leaving a wet trail in its wake. His silent way of showing that she was aroused, and he could continue. Oh frak, how could she want to run so badly and yet be so excited?

He returned to her pussy, a finger stroking through her folds. She kept waiting for groping, for his hand to rub her crotch as if sanding wood.

He didn't. Instead he used just a slickened fingertip, ever so slowly. Featherlight, it circled her clit, clockwise, then counter-clockwise, never actually touching the aching nubbin of nerves.

Her hips tried to push up, and the restraints held her completely still as his finger circled, then stroked down through her folds, making a figure eight, circling her opening, then up and around the increasingly sensitive nerves and back down in a rhythm that rolled through her like the ocean sounds rolled through her head.

She could actually feel her pussy swelling, engorging with blood until the tissues became painfully distended. Until...

Something touched her clit, right on top, a shocking warmth and wetness. She cried out, and the waves drowned the sound; she could only feel as his tongue stroked over her, lapping one side, then the other. Right over the top.

A seething tension grew inside her with every maddening, burning repetition.

He stopped, and then she felt something prodding at her opening. She drew in a breath, the muscles in her legs tightening. She knew this feeling. He was going to fuck her now, shove his cock in and—

It slid in, and she pulled in a breath at the exquisite feel of him sliding through her sensitive, swollen tissues. Her hands closed on the edge of the bench as the in-and-out movements sent her higher.

Then his cock somehow doubled in size, and his mouth came down on her clit again.

The piercing shock flamed through her. Her back arched, jostling the nipple clamps and sending electric sizzles to her pussy where his tongue flicked over her clit and his—not his cock, she realized with a startled breath—his fingers. He had his fingers in her and was pumping them slowly in and out as his tongue stroked her up and down.

The pace slowly increased, as did the wet pressure over her clit. His tongue drew an agonizing line of heat up one side as his fingers pushed deeper into her.

The sensations from his mouth and her insides merged, forming one desperate bundle of nerves. Another stroke of his tongue and slide of his fingers. Each ruthless touch sent her higher. The muscles in her vagina contracted until they ached, and her fingers scrabbled at the table as she tried to arch higher to his mouth. Needing, needing…

His tongue flicked directly on top of her clit.

The coiled-up ecstasy released as if launched from a cannon, shooting heat and pleasure through her in shattering spasms until her toes curled and her neck arched.

He licked over her again. And again. His fingers thrust deeply inside her, and her pussy clamped around him. She shuddered as more waves of pleasure broke over her helpless body.

When the fingers inside her could no longer elicit a quiver, he patted her thigh, and she felt the strap fall away. He did the other restraint and lowered her legs. For a minute, he massaged her aching muscles, and then he closed her thighs over her wet, swollen pussy, making her moan.

When he pulled the earphones off, all the noise of the club burst over her like a storm of sound.

"Look at me now, MacKensie."

She opened her eyes and stared into a gaze of molten blue. He stroked her hair back from her face, his lips curving in a faint smile.

He would want to get off very badly by now, she realized. He needed to take her, and she'd let him. He deserved it.

"I got off," she whispered, as if he didn't know. But she still couldn't believe it. Or what it had felt like, like the boundaries of her universe had expanded in the chaos of coming.

He nodded, his expression solemn, only a hint of laughter in his eyes. "I know."

She started to move and realized that her arms remained strapped down. "Why don't you release me?"

The dimple in his cheek grew as if he was smothering a laugh, and his eyes glinted. "Remember how I said I wouldn't hurt you?"

She nodded. A tremor moved through her body as she thought about all the whips and canes being used in this place.

"Well, I won't. But removing the breast clamps...might." And he undid the one on the left.

As blood surged back into the pinched nipple, nerves fired. *Painfully.* Her arms strained against the straps as she tried to touch the pain. And couldn't.

He smiled into her eyes before licking the throbbing nipple. Her back arched high, her arms held immobile, the sensation indescribable. As his tongue circled the swollen peak, the pain mingled with pleasure until she couldn't tell them apart.

"Brace yourself," he murmured. The second came off, and oh frak, it felt as if her nipple had ballooned into a huge, aching nerve. When he licked over the peak, a high whine escaped her.

A minute later, he released the rest of the straps and helped her off the table. Her knees buckled.

He caught her, picking her up easily. And carried her away from the table.

She stared up at him.

He'd had her tied up and available but hadn't taken her. He hadn't gotten off.

Chapter Eight

I got off.

Mac picked up a floppy-eared elephant and threw it across the yard. With a happy bark, Butler flew in pursuit, snatching it up before it had a chance to bounce, and pranced back to her, the elephant honking whenever his teeth pressed on the rubber nose.

She still couldn't get past the fact that she'd been horny and wet on Saturday night. God knew she'd tried before—okay, maybe not much—but she'd forced herself to accept dates in college. She'd gone out with men, had kissed men, and had even let them touch her until she couldn't stand having their hands on her any longer. No interest, no arousal, nothing.

But with *Alex*. She blew out an exasperated breath and pressed a hand over her quivering stomach. How had he done that to her? And *he* had accomplished it, not her. Surely not because he'd spanked her? Her automatic denial faded when she remembered how he'd held her down, how his hard hand had slapped her bottom, and how…strange…she'd felt.

Okay, maybe the spanking had something to do with how she reacted to him.

But the way he treated her had something to do with it also. He'd shown perfect control over himself—and her.

Bouncing with his excitement, Butler dropped the prize at her feet.

"What a good dog." She chose a duck from the toy box and let fly. Butler looked at the elephant on the ground—his favorite, she knew—and at the duck soaring across the yard. The duck won.

Mac leaned against the patio post, feeling like she'd aged about fifty years. Too much had happened over the past few days. Today—she'd spent today interviewing. Yesterday, Sunday, she'd escaped the house early and spent the day and evening sightseeing anywhere and everywhere she could think of. Anything to avoid talking with Alex.

Saturday? Well. She'd made an enemy, been attacked, been kissed. And had her first orgasm in well over twelve years. Her first one since she was a teenager and got herself there. She wrapped her arms around herself. Even the memory made her feel strange, as if she had turned into a stranger to herself.

Whores don't get off.

I'm not a whore.

But would that self-image ever go away? She'd only walked the streets of Des Moines for a year, and although feeling like an eternity, that time was just a small portion of her life. Then again, after the people in Jim's tiny town of Oak Hollow had discovered her past, they'd looked at her with revulsion. So, in a way, that one year had lasted many. Was it true that a person became what others thought of them?

Thud. Dancing a little, Butler acted like he'd brought her the stars and the moon. *What a cutie.* She hugged the stocky body and received a cursory lick on her neck before he stepped back, head lifted as if to say, *I'm busy here. Stay on task.*

She laughed and treated him to his elephant again. Later, when he'd worn out her throwing arm, she might be able to get him to snuggle against her.

Much as she'd snuggled against Alex Saturday night after he'd helped her off the table. He'd studied her face for a second, then picked her up and carried her to a quiet corner and just held her. He'd talked to her, but she didn't remember a word he'd said, just the sound of his deep voice.

Later that night, she'd sat up in her bed and stared at the flowery wall illumined by the nightlight she'd taken from the bathroom. And remembered again. *Alex hadn't gotten off.*

That still seemed the most unreal part of the event.

Butler barked sharply, and Mac jumped. The Lab gave her an exasperated look and pointed his nose at the elephant lying on her shoes.

"Sorry, baby." She took the elephant from Butler and put it into the toy box. "I'm done. Can I bribe you with a dog cookie?" she asked, bending to stroke his head.

At the club, Alex had concentrated on giving her pleasure. That just wasn't normal. What kind of a man was he? She straightened, shook her head, and ran right into Alex, bouncing off a chest as solid as a concrete wall.

He chuckled as he grabbed her upper arms to steady her. "Sorry, pet. I didn't realize you hadn't heard me."

She looked up into his blue eyes. The ocean sounds from Saturday night seemed to fill her ears, and this time she felt caught in a riptide, pulled helplessly...somewhere. "Um. Right. We...we were just playing."

He smiled, took her face between his hands, and kissed her gently. His lips still held that tantalizing, velvety firmness.

When he stepped back, she knew her heart had sped up.

Alex stroked his thumb over her soft lips. Pretty little sub, all flushed and confused. If she were anyone else, were a normal submissive living in his household, he'd strip her down and take her right now. Maybe lash her hands to the unobtrusive rings he'd bolted into the pillars, lift her legs, and...

He smiled down into her big brown eyes and squeezed her shoulders instead, enjoying the tremor that ran through her at his touch. He'd pushed her hard at the club, taking advantage of how the attack had lowered her defenses and, even better, her unexpected bout of jealousy. She'd responded beyond his expectations, but he could see she was shaken to the core. The little sub had pain buried in her, deep hurts and scars. His job as a Dom was to expose and help her deal with them, but she—

"Why didn't you stay with Cynthia?" she asked, breaking into his thoughts. "She's beautiful."

"A good question, but first let's find something to eat." He took her hand and pulled her into the kitchen. "Margaret should have restocked the refrigerator today." And she had. The refrigerator held a pan of lasagna. Alex set the oven and tucked the dish in, looking forward to the meal. Margaret made a fine lasagna.

Showing a pleasing stubborn streak, MacKensie insisted they make a fruit salad to tide them over until the lasagna could bake. She shoved an apple and knife over to his half of the island and then started cutting up strawberries. Her delicate hands handled the knife with terrifying competence, reminding him that a veterinarian was also a surgeon.

Mac was skillful, stubborn, assertive, and so insecure that she'd stayed away from the house all of yesterday, coming in late enough that she could merely nod at him without meeting his gaze. He'd given her the space and time to think things out, and obviously she felt more on an even keel today.

"Cynthia?" she reminded him, scooping her pile into the salad bowl.

"Cynthia is beautiful," he agreed. "Clever, rich, and charming when she wants to be. She's also self-centered and"—he waggled the apple—"rotten on the inside." Her indifference to anyone's pain and problems disgusted him.

"But you were together?"

"'Together' isn't the correct term." He held a piece of apple to MacKensie's mouth and grinned when she gave the fruit a suspicious glance before accepting it. Did she realize how much a Dom enjoyed hand-feeding his sub?

He continued. "She knows that I don't get involved with anyone. As for dating her, I topped her once at the club and served as her Dom at a few parties. She never spent the night here; I've never entered her apartment."

"Oh." Mac accepted another bite. "Considering how much she wants you, she surely put her best foot forward. But you didn't date her long, so how did you know she's a bad apple?"

Alex smiled. Even a Dom could be blinded to a person's motivations, at least at first, and in trying to avoid women just after his money, he'd ended up with Cynthia. In escaping from Cynthia, he got this little cat with all sorts of problems, but who considered taking his money to be an affront to her pride. Definitely a leap up.

He watched her cut up another strawberry, the blade flashing. Tiny hands, fragile wrists, yet he could see the muscles in her bare arms. Her breasts were well concealed under a white button-down shirt, her legs hidden under a tailored skirt. Interview clothes. So very tidy. Time to muss her up a little and remind her she could be aroused.

After she tossed the last fruit slices into the bowl, he grasped her around the waist, enjoying the tiny gasp, and set her on a clean place on the island. Pushing her skirt up, he edged between her legs.

"What are you doing?" The pupils in her brown eyes had dilated, and her voice turned husky.

He ran his hands along her legs, over her firm ass, up her waist, and stopped just under her breasts. "I wanted to remember how your body feels under my hands," he murmured.

"Alex." She caught his hands and held them in front of her. Her mouth firmed into a straight line, showing the stubborn line of her jaw.

"More worries, little sub?" he asked, expecting to hear the "no sex" objection.

"You don't know me. Not at all." Her small body tightened. "I'm not a nice person either. You wouldn't like me once... Um, you wouldn't like me."

So many fears. How did someone so competent and caring acquire such self-doubt? "MacKensie."

She stilled at his growl.

"Let me tell you what I see, sweetheart. Your core"—he pressed his open palm between her breasts, felt her rapid breathing—"the heart of you is sweet. Loving. Tender." He smiled. Did she realize he'd watched Butler suck her into throwing the chew toys for far longer than most people would have tolerated? He'd seen the hugs and kisses and seen Butler's adoration. Butler liked anyone who got past his guard and petted him. But he reserved his adoration for a very few special people.

"I, of course, checked your recommendations and records. You're incredibly intelligent, with a fine education and a solid reputation as a vet."

Her fingers relaxed, and her eyes widened. Surprise and...pleasure. Did no one in her life compliment her? He no longer wondered if she'd experienced abuse in the past; he just wanted to know what kind.

Childhood pain seemed likely. But that business with arousal... Had she been raped? The way her body had tensed on the bench when he'd put a finger into her vagina... Had she expected pain or humiliation?

No matter right now. He'd pushed her at the club. Time to go easy. He pulled her shirt loose from the skirt and slid his hands under the shirt and up her back.

She inhaled, her muscles tensing, her spine straightening. Her hands gripped his shoulders, her fingers digging into his muscles in her instinctive reaction to a man's hands on her body. "We're not... This isn't a club or party," she said, her voice unsteady.

"You're very observant," he said. He was observant as well; she hadn't said no, and her protest had been more for form's sake. She wanted his touch—and feared it at the same time. So he ignored the rigidity of her muscles and simply pleased himself, running his hands over her bared skin in a subtle reminder that her body was available to him. Those toned muscles under silky-soft skin were a delight to a Dom's hands. He continued, keeping his touch only on her waist, never venturing near her breasts or under her skirt.

The tiny hands on his shoulders relaxed, and her breathing slowed as the lack of threat let her enjoy his touch.

Then, with a smothered sigh of regret, he removed his hands, pulled her shirt down, and set her on her feet. "Let's eat on the patio."

A week of interviews. Could there be anything more stressful in the entire world than having strangers grill you about anything and everything? Too tired to climb the stairs to her room, Mac went through the house to the back. She stepped out onto the patio and stretched, trying to relieve the knots in her shoulders.

No one had offered her a position yet. She huffed a laugh. She'd actually had this vague hope that she'd walk into a clinic and they'd jump up from behind a desk and give her a job. Maybe even a partnership. Apparently they hadn't read that script. The vets who had interviewed her had been polite, but they had others to interview and credentials to check.

Sad to say, she didn't have a huge number of references to wave in front of them. Aside from the vet who'd bought Jim's clinic, the only names on her list came from college. But they were glowing recommendations at least. Since her instructors hadn't known her past, they'd judged her only on competence. *And I'm damned competent.*

A scramble of feet came from inside the house, and Butler charged out, a good eighty-or-so pounds of enthusiasm. Turning in circles so he could lick and get petted both, he knocked her back a step. Bracing herself, she giggled. How could she stay unhappy with this bundle of joy around?

"He missed you," Alex said, stepping out the door.

God, just look at him. Dark tailored slacks, silky white shirt with the sleeves rolled up to display strong arms and lean hands. The top few buttons were undone, and her gaze caught on the hollow at the base of his throat surrounded by corded muscles.

Each night this week they'd had supper together, talked, watched TV. He'd kissed her and touched her, but never intimately. She'd changed the bandages on his back and tried to ignore how…pleasant…his bare skin felt under her fingers. She couldn't help but remember how his fingers had stroked her…entered her.

And now her fingers tingled with the need to touch him. To be touched. And wasn't that a bizarre feeling? When she met his gaze, she could see the amusement in his eyes, so she bent over to pet Butler some more and get her body under control.

He found this so simple. Women undoubtedly threw themselves at his feet—literally, she thought, thinking of Cynthia. But for her… The first time she'd really looked at a man in years and he had to be some all-powerful Dom. Rich, handsome, exuding confidence. If she'd actually planned to try a man-woman relationship, she'd have chosen someone nice. Kind. Easy. Not someone who—

Firm hands closed around her wrists, anchoring them behind her back as Alex pulled her up against him. He kissed her, teasing, lazy kisses, his mouth gentle, his body hard, and his grip ruthless. The mixture made her head spin. Her insides seemed to melt into a pool, and her balance disappeared as he coaxed her into more: into deeper, into wetter, into hotter. When he pulled back, her nipples ached, and her pussy felt as swollen as her lips.

He brushed his lips over hers, then nipped her chin, and the tiny pain awakened more urgency inside her. "I missed you too, pet," he murmured.

With a whine, Butler stepped on her feet, trying to get closer.

Alex let her go and leaned against the patio table. "Do you have any interviews this weekend?"

"No." Unnerved by the heaviness in her limbs, she knelt to scratch Butler's sides, sending him into a frenzy of delight.

"The newscasters predict sunny skies tomorrow, although there's no guarantee with Washington weather. I thought we'd host a few people at the Vashon Island house."

"Vashon Island?"

"In the center of Puget Sound, just a ferry ride away." He smiled. "Don't worry, little Midwesterner, you'll like it. You haven't even visited the beach yet, have you?"

The thrill of seeing an island diminished as the rest of his plans registered. *Host. Few people.* "What kind of people?" she asked suspiciously.

"*Those* kind of people. A few whips, a chain or two. A house party tends to be more casual than the club, although we'll undoubtedly indulge in some evil play with our subs." He chuckled at her flinch. "Yes, that will include you, pet. We won't leave until noon, so you can sleep in."

She swallowed and nodded, wrapping her arms around Butler, although who comforted whom, she wasn't sure.

"Relax, little cat. That's tomorrow. Not here yet." Bending down, Alex tucked a strand of hair behind her ear and smiled at her, his eyes crinkling. "Tonight, you deserve a reward for surviving all those interviews. I ordered us a pizza with everything on it."

"Really?" When they'd shopped for her clothes, they'd wandered past a pizza place, fragrant with tomato sauce and melted cheese. She'd mentioned that she'd always rewarded herself for good grades with a fully loaded pizza.

Just an off-the-cuff comment...but he'd remembered.

Chapter Nine

I t promised to be an interesting—and miserable—evening. Alex pushed open a window overlooking the Sound and let the breeze dry his body. The waves frothed over the sand, reminding him of the afternoon and the enchanted expression on his little sub's face. He'd enjoyed the way she'd immersed herself in the feel of the sand on her bare feet, the gentle movement of the water, the smell of the sea brine. Even the sandpipers running down the beach, the hermit crabs scuttling around under stolen shells, and the seagulls circling had received her absorbed attention.

He hadn't heard her truly laugh before, but when Butler raced after the gulls, sending them squawking into the air, her laughter escaped, clear and melodic. Free of restraint. Later, when he'd coaxed her back to the house, her face had been colored pink from sunburn and wind, and every tense line had disappeared.

Damn, but he wanted to hear her laugh like that again and see her eyes free of shadows.

He sighed and toweled off his hair. Instead the evening would be stressful, especially for her, but he couldn't refuse Drake's request. As the injured party, MacKensie needed to witness this, even if she'd rather not. He tossed the towel over a chair and pulled on black jeans.

The little vet was a compassionate woman. And an honest woman. Alex still hadn't figured out why she'd broken into the dungeon, but he'd found no lack of character in her nature. She'd held to their bargain despite her qualms.

In all reality, her transgression hadn't been that great, and her trip to his club should have served as full repayment and punishment. If she'd been anyone else, he'd have released her at that point.

But his little sub would have disappeared from his life. He knew that. And when he'd taken her under his command, he'd become obligated to more than fairness. If he could accomplish nothing with her problems, then he'd step away. But she'd given him her trust and more. He snorted at the masculine satisfaction welling inside him. Her first orgasm in twelve years—or maybe even longer? She had said twelve years for sex, not for a climax.

In the master bath, the jets shut off.

As Alex buttoned his shirt, Mac walked out, flushed pink and swathed in one of the oversize terry-cloth robes he kept at the beach house. Her scent—vanilla, citrus, and woman—drifted to him, and he hooked an arm around her waist, ignoring her squeak.

"You smell edible, little sub," he murmured. Wishing he could toss her on the bed and bury his face between her legs, he settled for shoving her robe off her shoulder and nuzzling the juncture of her neck and shoulder. Moist skin, soft. He bit down on the muscle there, and he felt a quiver run through her. When he slid his hand inside the robe, her nipples were already bunching.

With a sigh of regret, he smiled into her outraged yet already aroused gaze. "Your outfit is on the bed. Wear it all—and nothing else, pet. I'll see you downstairs."

After savoring one last caress of the tiny peaked nipples, he released her. He'd kept his touch casual all week; her break was over. By the time he finished tonight, he intended to see those peaks swollen to twice the size, dark red, and rigid.

✦ ✦ ✦ ✦

Dressed as ordered, Mac walked into the living room and stopped to survey the situation. Alex was building a fire in the fireplace across the room. Just behind him on the couch, Zachary, a gray-haired rancher, sat with his red-haired sub in his lap.

Over by the wall of windows, Peter, a lean blond lawyer, and his sub, Hope, watched the last remnants of pink disappear from Mount Rainier. Mac vaguely remembered meeting the two at the club. Short and round, with freckles and an infectious giggle, Hope seemed far too cute for her serious Dom.

Mac was the only sub dressed in a costume. Four years of college, vet school, interning—all those years and here she was, attired in a fancy and very revealing maid's outfit. *Go figure.*

Halfway across the room to the others, she stopped. *Why am I doing this anyway?* Frowning, she walked up to Alex. "Could I speak with you for a moment?" She added a reluctant "Sir" when his eyebrows rose.

"Excuse us," he said to the others before walking with her out onto the deck.

Mac leaned over the railing and looked down. The beach below had an eerie gleam from the moon rising in the east, and the water glimmered as small waves rolled onto the sand.

"Did you have a question for me, little vet?" Alex set a warm hand on her shoulder and turned her to face him.

"Yes. Obviously Cynthia isn't a problem for you any longer, so why am I still pretending to be your submissive?"

Silence.

The pause worried her. Darkness shadowed Alex's face, and she couldn't read his expression. "You have two parts to your question, MacKensie," he said finally. "First, we are not yet finished with Cynthia. I can promise you that." His voice had a grim quality that made her shiver.

His voice deepened. "Second." He tangled his hand in her loose hair and pulled her head back, putting her fully in the light streaming from the glass door. "Are you really pretending, little one? When I do this"—he took a step forward, pressing his body against hers, immobilizing her against the railing, and holding her hair so she was forced to stare up at him—"are you insulted and annoyed? Or does something in you shiver?"

With his body against hers, he couldn't help but feel the tremor that ran through her. Still holding her hair captive, he took her lips roughly, demanding and possessive.

The heat sweeping through her body turned to fire when his hand captured her breast. Too many sensations hit her at once: his mouth possessing hers, his powerful body trapping her, his hand on her breast, the thumb scraping over her tightening nipple. By the time he pulled back, she'd been thoroughly kissed. And thoroughly aroused.

He studied her face before stepping back and letting her free. "Our bargain stands. You may go back in." He motioned politely to the door.

Her legs unsteady, she reentered the room. Damn. Her face heated as she realized how she must look: tousled and turned on. God knew, she felt turned on, and wasn't that a strange sensation?

A rap on the front door interrupted her thoughts. Were they expecting more people? "I'll get this one, pet," Alex said, patting her bottom on the way past.

When he opened the door, Mac backed up a step, her breath catching in her throat. Steel, the Dom who'd attacked her, stood there with a big black bag slung over his shoulder and wearing battered leathers that left his chest completely bare.

He saw her standing frozen in the center of the room. "Relax, girl. I'm not here for you." He glanced at Alex. "Definitely a pretty sub."

"I think so." Alex raised his voice to the other guests. "This is Steel, who will handle the evening's punishment."

As he and Steel moved into the living room, Mac retreated, trying to find an unobtrusive spot to hide.

"Sit here with me." Curled in one corner of the couch by the windows, Hope patted the cushion beside her.

Mac glanced around. Over by the fireplace, Peter and Zachary shook hands with Steel, while Tess sat nearby listening.

"Thanks." Mac dropped down on the couch beside Hope. "I-I don't know why that man is here. Alex didn't even know him until..." How could she ever explain what had happened in the club?

"Until he attacked you. Peter told me. He said all the Doms are furious about it, and that's why that guy is here."

"I don't understand."

Another knock on the door. Alex strode across the room to answer it.

Mac shook her head, a little dismayed. "Alex called this a really little party, just you guys and—" Her mouth dropped open when Cynthia walked in, hands cuffed in front of her. A man in a black silk suit followed. Probably a few years older than Alex, his black hair was shorter, and gray flecked his neatly trimmed mustache.

"My God, that's Drake," Hope whispered.

The man named Drake removed the long coat draped over Cynthia's shoulders. He tossed it over the table by the front door and pointed to an empty corner. Eyes down, the tall brunette walked over and knelt, facing the wall.

He and Alex talked for a moment, and then they both crossed the room toward Mac.

When Hope slid off the couch onto her knees, Mac gave her a puzzled look but did the same. *Don't look at strange Doms.* Mac remembered that rule, so she kept her gaze firmly on the floor. A pair of dress shoes and black trousers stepped into her narrow focus. Alex wore boots. This must be Drake, standing over her.

He'd brought Cynthia. Why? And why did everyone—including Alex—look so grim?

"Hope, return to your master." Drake's voice was as deep as Alex's, but with a faint European accent and as smooth as cream. Yet the smoothness was like a film of snow over a mountain range, barely covering the power.

Hope scrambled to her feet and escaped, for escape was totally what it looked like.

"Permission?" Drake said.

"Granted." Alex's voice. Mac's hands fisted at her sides. Cynthia, Steel, and Drake, who frightened sweet Hope. What was going on?

"MacKensie." That ever-so-suave voice gave the end of her name a slight fillip. "Eyes on me."

She looked up. Drake held his hand out to her. After a second, she let him pull her to her feet. He stood a couple of inches taller than Alex, and with a man on each side of her, she felt far too much like a bug about to be squashed.

"My name is Drake." His eyes were as black as his hair. She wanted to step back, but he still had her hand. She glanced at Alex helplessly.

He stepped to her side as if hearing her plea for rescue. "Shhh, little cat. Drake isn't here to upset you." He scooped her up in his arms, pulling her away from Drake, and sat down on the couch. "So stop upsetting her, you intimidating bastard," he said.

Rather than striking Alex dead somehow—she didn't know how, but he looked like he could—Drake gave a deep laugh and took the other end of the couch. Her sigh of relief faded when he held his hand out to her again. He waited, palm up in a silent demand, until she'd given him hers. But Alex held her now, and somehow that made everything better.

Drake's hand was warm and dry, firm, with oddly placed calluses. "MacKensie, I own Chains." He glanced at Alex with a glimmer of a smile. "A few friends invested, but the ultimate authority is mine. You were victimized in my club. Although I can't remove the memory, I must try to make it right."

He nodded toward Cynthia, who still knelt in the corner. "After the barmaid identified her, a friend in the police force matched her fingerprints to the ones on the note. I wanted to turn her over to the police, but..." He sighed and rubbed his chin.

MacKensie tried to pull her hand away. Obviously the rich, beautiful Cynthia had either cried or bought him off or—

"The club operates under very stringent rules of privacy," Drake said, interrupting her unspoken tirade. "To convict her would require a trial and witnesses. You would have to take the stand."

Mac's mouth dropped open. "Me?" She hadn't thought it through at all.

Drake tilted his head. "Alex said you're starting a career here. He doubted you'd want to be identified as having visited a BDSM club, let alone having had an altercation like this one."

"Oh God, no." A whole new life and reputation ruined.

"Good call, then." The black gaze flickered to Alex before returning to her. "So we were left in a quandary. To have undermined the lifestyle in such a calculated way and to have instigated such a cruel act—such behavior cannot be permitted. So Cynthia received a choice."

Mac could feel her hand trembling in his grasp; so could he, for he covered her fingers with his other hand.

"Either arrest and prosecution to the full extent of the law— or she could receive exactly what she had planned for you. Willingly." His eyes rested on Cynthia for a moment, and Mac shivered at the merciless look in them.

He gave Mac a faint smile. "Cynthia has no idea that you wouldn't enjoy publicly shaming her in court and destroying the social standing that means so much to her. So she signed not only a confession but an agreement to make things right. She and Steel are here tonight so that you, as the injured party, as well as Alex, can bear witness."

"She could receive exactly what she had planned." Mac didn't want to think about Steel's actions, but would he have stopped at whipping her? What would have been the inevitable conclusion of that scene?

"No," Mac whispered. "No rape." She tried to straighten up against the painful clenching in her stomach. "I don't want that for her. Not for anyone."

"You know your sub well, don't you?" Drake nodded to Alex, a glint of amusement in his eyes. Lifting Mac's hand, he kissed her fingers. "You have a soft heart, *chérie*. It shall be as you wish." His mouth thinned. "However, the whipping is nonnegotiable."

Chapter Ten

H is little sub was warm and soft in Alex's arms, content to be held as Drake walked over to Steel and spoke with him briefly. When Steel crossed the room and grabbed Cynthia by the hair, Mac's eyes went wide with distress.

Alex tightened his arms. "Shhh."

Steel pulled Cynthia to her feet, and the brunette cringed when she realized who would dispense her punishment. "No!"

"'Fraid so, girl. Let's get this over with." Steel marched her to where Drake held open the door to the small dungeon. After nodding at Steel, Drake closed the soundproofed door behind the two and walked over to join the other Doms.

"MacKensie," Alex said quietly, "I didn't think you'd want to watch. But if you do—"

"No." Mac shuddered and buried her head in his shoulder.

Satisfaction washed through him like a warm wave; she had learned to look to him for comfort. He stroked her fair hair, silky strands over satin skin. "Then there is nothing we need to do now." But from the continued tenseness in her body, he realized she was listening, fearing to hear the whip or Cynthia. "The room is soundproofed, little cat. You can't hear anything."

"Oh."

But she'd listen anyway. Carrying her in his arms, he joined the group around the fireplace and took the empty chair across from Drake. Every sub had reacted in exactly the same way as his. On the couch, Peter held Hope in his arms, and Tess sat on the floor between Zachary's legs with his hands massaging her shoulders. The Doms all had the same grim look in their eyes, even Drake.

The punishment had to be done, but no one was pleased about it. And everyone was listening.

"Little cat," Alex murmured. "Would you put on some music for me? Maybe Enya? I'm going to serve drinks."

"Yes, Sir," she whispered.

He held her still so he could smile at her. "I like the way that sounds. You please me, MacKensie."

A flush bloomed in her pale face in response to his approval.

By the time he'd finished making up everyone's usual drink, the soft sounds of Enya filled the room.

Drake smiled slightly when Alex handed him the scotch he favored. "You're a good host, and this is an excellent diversion. Thank you." He took a small sip, then put the glass down.

Alex took the last two drinks off the tray and reclaimed his chair. He set the drinks on the small table and held his arms out, pleased when MacKensie burrowed back into his embrace without hesitation. He handed her a gin and tonic and picked up his scotch, then glanced at Drake. "You think this will be the end of it?"

Drake frowned. "As far as copycats, yes. I gave Steel a camera for before-and-after photos. Although I'll black out her face, Cynthia's body is quite recognizable, and the story of what she did is making the rounds. When the pictures from tonight are posted over the bar, I doubt anyone will consider duplicating what she did."

The talk turned general, and the Doms encouraged the subs to join in to keep their minds off the scene being played out in the dungeon.

Zachary told how his new ram had butted him off his feet; Tess teased the rancher about the dungeon he'd built in the barn.

Hope had several troublesome students creating chaos in her classroom. Peter suffered from a backlogged caseload that kept him working late each night.

"You know, we never asked how you met," Hope said, smiling at Mac.

MacKensie stirred in Alex's arms. "We exchanged houses. Butler needed someone to care for him while Alex attended some conference close to my hometown." She frowned and looked up at him. "After seeing your house, I couldn't believe you wanted to use my little place."

"I've found staying in a real house—even little ones—more comfortable than any motel room. And it's worth the drive if I can get out of the city and enjoy a smaller town."

"Oh." MacKensie returned her attention to Hope. "Anyway, he missed his flight and returned to the house."

And found her in a wonderful position. Alex grinned as red streaked across MacKensie's face. She obviously hadn't forgotten either. "She was nice enough to let me stay in my own home."

He heard the little sigh of relief that he hadn't gone into detail.

With a little *click*, the music came to an end. Mac turned toward the dungeon. "Why isn't he done?"

"Steel was furious he'd been used in such a way," Drake said. "And he's a master with the single tail. He won't break skin, but she will be marked for quite some time."

"You must love her a lot to punish her like this," Mac said.

Alex frowned at the peculiar statement and realized there was something odd in her voice. Wistfulness? Envy?

His glance at the others silenced them. "What other punishment could we have used, little cat?" Alex asked softly.

Her hand resting on his chest curled into a small fist. "If you didn't like her, you'd put her out of sight. Send her where you didn't have to look at her."

Such a matter-of-fact statement. A reality to MacKensie. Alex frowned as dawning comprehension created a knot in his stomach. "So Cynthia knows we love her, since we're whipping her raw?"

Her cheek rubbed against his shirt as if she were the little cat he called her. Even as she snuggled, a frown formed between her brows. "I don't know about whipping. It seems awfully harsh."

"I guess we could have flogged her." He paused. No response. "Or caned her." Paused. "Or spanked her."

MacKensie's breathing increased, and the tiny muscles in her lips quivered for a second.

"Yes, maybe a hard spanking. Would she know what it meant, though?" He threw that out blindly and got more than he'd anticipated.

"Only girls who are loved get spanked. She'd know that." Again, a reasonable tone. Spanking and love went together in MacKensie's world, a thought pattern probably established so young, she didn't even realize it. He'd dig further. But for now she needed to know she was valued as much—more—than Cynthia. He could give her that. With a little help.

He glanced at Peter and Zachary, saw the understanding in their eyes, and received nods. Experienced Doms could no more ignore a need like this than a doctor could ignore a bleeding wound.

The dungeon door opened, and Steel walked out, his hand wrapped around Cynthia's upper arm, giving her support enough to walk, but from the repugnance in his face, he didn't want to get closer. Steel's mouth was tight; he obviously hadn't enjoyed the punishment, but he'd done a masterful job.

Red welts covered Cynthia's body, front and back, shoulders to calves, only the areas around her kidneys and spine left unmarked. Her tear-streaked makeup splotched her face like camo paint, and her eyes were glassy with pain.

Pity rose in Alex until he remembered that she'd tried to do the same to Mac for no other reason than spite.

When the two approached, Drake rose. His black eyes displayed no pity at all as they traveled over Cynthia's body. "Kneel and apologize to Master Steel, then to Master Alex's sub." His words were deliberately chosen, and Cynthia flinched at MacKensie's designation as Alex's submissive.

Cynthia knelt awkwardly, all her grace gone. "I'm sorry, Master Steel. Please forgive me." The monotone left little to be read.

"Forgiven," Steel said, his taut face adding without words that he wouldn't forget.

Cynthia turned slightly and looked at MacKensie. "Please forgive me," she repeated, her face blank and cold.

MacKensie's eyes brimmed with tears. "Of course," she whispered.

Alex's mouth thinned. His little sub's sympathy could be heard, felt, and seen. Cynthia's attitude, however…

"Cynthia, you speak the words of repentance but feel no remorse, only unhappiness that you were caught," Drake said and lifted Cynthia to her feet. "You are not welcome in my club. Do not return."

The woman's soft gasp of shock showed she had expected everything would go back to normal.

Drake handed Steel his car keys. "Please escort her to the car. I will be out in a moment."

Steel nodded and gripped Cynthia's arm again. He snagged her coat on the way out the door.   —

Drake walked over to Alex. A flick of his eyes asked for and received Alex's permission to speak and touch. He lifted MacKensie's chin with one finger. "Little one, a truly repentant submissive is forgiven and cherished by her master, whether she is punished or not." His black eyes gentled as if he could feel the quivers racking the little cat's body. "And sometimes punishment isn't about love; sometimes it's just punishment."

He let her go, nodded at Alex, and headed out to take Cynthia home. Alex didn't envy him the trip.

"I think the evening calls for a walk on the beach," Alex said. "Come, people; let's get some fresh air." He set his mostly untouched drink down on the table. There was yet a scene to play out tonight, and he'd need a clear head.

✧ ✧ ✧ ✧ ✧

Seattle glowed brightly on the horizon as Mac took one last look before entering the house. The long walk in the brisk sea air had blown away the shadows of the evening, and the soft shushing of the waves erased the screams that had filled her imagination. Alex had held her hand as they strolled along the water's edge, and that had helped too. Mostly.

So maybe she'd had a few moments of wanting to be home, reading an old Heinlein, and snuggling in the extra-soft quilt that Mary had made just for her—the one with kittens peeking out from behind each square. The homesickness hadn't lasted too long. Hand on her stomach, Mac rubbed away the lingering remnants and took a fortifying breath of cool, briny air.

After tossing their coats on the entry table, the others headed into the kitchen. Tess said she'd make some hot chocolate and asked Alex where he kept the Baileys Irish Cream. Sounded like everyone felt better.

Oblivious to the subdued mood, Butler had spent his time running in happy circles on the moonlit beach, and now he trotted up to the house, sides heaving and tongue lolling out.

Before he could escape, Mac grabbed his collar. As she pulled the dog toward the back room to dry him off, she heard Peter's voice in the kitchen. "Push her?"

Alex answered, "Exactly."

Push her? Push who and where and why? Those Doms could be pretty inscrutable sometimes. With a shrug, Mac concentrated on getting the seawater and sand off Butler and not on herself.

"I do not want to smell like fish and dog," she told him, receiving wiggles of delight at the attention. She put out some more dry food, checked his water, and left him tromping down imaginary grasses to make his dog bed more comfy.

Mac stopped in the hall to remove her long coat, then entered the living room. Everyone had returned to their favorite locations: Zachary and Tess in front of the fire, Peter and Hope at the large picture window, watching the water. Alex appeared from the kitchen with a large tray of appetizers. "Ah, my favorite French maid. Serve our guests, please." He handed her the tray.

She glanced down at her costume and sighed. She'd actually forgotten what she wore, and now she knew why he'd wanted her to wear it. With a soft laugh, she walked over to Hope and Peter. "Would you care for something to eat?"

Peter's brows drew together, and his light brown eyes chilled. "Has Alex not taught you how to address a Dom?"

Oh frak. Where'd all the friendly atmosphere go? "Ah. Sir. Would you care for something to eat, Sir?"

"Better." Peter picked up tidbits, one by one, and popped them into Hope's mouth while Mac stood as if she'd turned into a table or something. After a few minutes, Peter finished feeding his sub and took a miniature quiche for himself. As he ate it, he looked Mac up and down, making her very aware of the scantiness of her costume. She tried to think of a way to edge away, but that would be too obvious. Instead she turned her gaze to the water. *I'm a table. Just a table.*

Knuckles caressed the top of Mac's pushed-up breasts, and she jumped, almost spilling the appetizers. She tried to step away, but Peter grasped her arm, holding her in place. He ran his hand over her cleavage again. When she glared at him, he smiled slowly. "If maids don't pay attention, they get in trouble. Didn't your master mention that?"

She frowned at him, getting a feeling there was no right answer.

"At this party—at most of our parties—we grant permission for the other Doms to touch our subs. Within reason." The back of his hand stroked over her neck and bare shoulders.

Alex hadn't, had he? She looked over her shoulder to where he stood by the fireplace, his arm resting on the thick oak mantel. His blue gaze met hers. After glancing at Peter, he returned to his conversation. Dammit. An ugly burn ignited in her stomach, and it sure wasn't arousal. Obviously Peter had permission to touch her. How far could he and the other Dom go? "What is considered within reason?" she asked and hastily added, "Sir."

He tugged on her hair. "Well, now, that changes with each party. Right now, I think I'll improve the view." His fingers slid inside her corset, and she tried to jerk away. "Don't move, sub," he snapped. His eyes, so light a brown they were almost gold, seemed to glow.

She froze, and the tray she held started to shake. He took the tray and set it onto the table, then, watching her with a steady gaze, undid a few of her corset hooks, exposing her breasts down to the nipples. Her hands fisted at her sides in an effort not to push him away.

With an amused smile that reminded her of Alex's, he handed her the tray. "Off with you now, pet. I'm sure Master Zachary is hungry. Ranchers like their food."

She stopped halfway across the room, trying to get her composure back. Somehow, when she'd been a whore, she'd managed to turn off her sense of outrage. Not tonight. Peter's touch hadn't roused her like Alex's; instead he'd made her angry. *What a jerk.*

She eyed her gaping corset and tried to decide whether to set the tray down and do the hooks back up or continue serving. Glancing over her shoulder, she saw Peter's steady gaze on her, so she gripped the tray firmly and soldiered on. Hopefully the rancher would be more polite.

Zachary sat on the couch. Feet tucked under her long skirt, Tess curled up against him. The Dom had a craggy, weathered face with darkly tanned skin like a man who'd spent his life outdoors. When Mac offered him the tray, rather than sitting up and selecting something, he remained leaning back, one arm along the back of the couch.

Mac held the tray forward.

"Down here, where I can see what I'm getting," he ordered, pointing toward his lap.

Well, good grief. Does Alex know what voyeurs his friends are? She bent over, all too aware of how the weight of her breasts made the corset gape farther open.

He did the exact same as Peter, picking out appetizers and feeding them to Tess. While Mac remained bent over.

"You know, that corset looks mighty uncomfortable." Zachary ran a finger along the top. "Don't move," he cautioned. He reached over the tray and undid hooks until only three remaining clasps at the bottom and the two thin shoulder straps kept it on her body. "There, that should feel better."

She glared at him.

He smiled slowly, but no humor showed. From the corner of her eye, Mac saw his sub ease away from him. With one finger, Zachary lifted Mac's chin, forcing her gaze to stay on him. "MacKensie. I don't like that look."

She yanked her face away and stepped back. "Well, I don't like—"

He rose so fast, she didn't have time to move. Yanked from her hands, the tray hit the table with a clatter, and Mac landed facedown on the couch with a hard hand keeping her in place. A second later, he'd stripped her of the corset entirely, leaving her in only a thong, garter belt, and fishnet stockings.

Before she could think what to do, Zachary set her on her feet and took his place back on the couch. He wasn't even breathing fast. "I realize you're a beginner, so I let you off lightly." He handed her the tray. "You may take that to your master and explain why you're not in uniform any longer."

She stared at him, her heart hammering in her chest. He'd taken her clothing. But he hadn't tried to cop a feel, not like most men would have. And although his eyes showed appreciation for her nakedness, he made no move to touch her further. He was totally in control. She took a step back, caught a sympathetic look from Tess, and kept retreating. Damn him.

No way…no way was she going to walk essentially naked all evening. Especially with everyone else fully dressed. She looked around for Alex. His back to the room, he pointed out something on the water to Peter. Mac glanced at Zachary. He'd pulled Tess into his lap to kiss her. No one watched Mac. And the door was right there.

She might not surrender, but she'd definitely retreat.

Chapter Eleven

fter setting the tray down, Mac hastened up the stairs to the master bedroom. And there she paced, caught in a quandary. Should she return back downstairs for the rest of the party? Damned if she would do that without clothing. But if she put on clothes, what would Zachary do? Even scarier, what would *Alex* do? Her heart squeezed at the thought of his displeasure, and wasn't that totally bizarre? In the last twelve years, aside from Jim and Mary, she'd never changed her behavior for anyone, no matter what they might think.

Okay, Mac. Think. Be logical. If she didn't go back downstairs, she'd break the deal with Alex. She'd promised to submit at his parties and all that. This was a party. So she couldn't cut out early, no matter how offensive his guests were.

But she refused to walk around without clothing, so... Her suitcase held a long jean skirt like Tess's and a discreet, sleeveless, button-down top. After pulling them on, she checked herself in the mirror. Nothing provocative about this.

Surely Alex would understand that she couldn't tolerate being mostly naked. Wouldn't he?

Frak, but I'm so screwed. Trying to rub the butterflies out of her stomach, she descended the stairs and entered the living room. The light scent of wood smoke from the fire mingled with a cool breeze from the window someone had opened. Zachary and Tess had joined the others at the window, so everyone stood on one side of the room. Mac clenched her hands at her sides. Join them or resume serving? But she'd already served them once, dammit, and look how well that had turned out.

Casual, then. Just go hang out with them. *Note to self: stay a good distance away from the nasty Doms.*

Her breath kept hitching like a bad motor as she crossed the room and stopped beside Alex. Eyes down like a good little sub, she listened to Tess's description of kayaking. When Tess's light voice stopped in midsentence, no one picked up the conversation.

Silence grew.

Mac glanced out of the corner of her eye at Tess and Hope. The look of horror blossoming on their faces made her stomach sink. *Oh frak. Beam me up, Scotty. Quick.*

A hand closed around her bare arm in a firm grip. *Alex.* He turned her toward him.

Her hands closed into fists, but she kept her gaze on the floor, at least until his finger under her chin raised her gaze to his.

Cold, cold eyes, like blue ice. "I seem to recall putting you in a maid's outfit." His voice had deepened, but he spoke softly. "Why are you not wearing it, MacKensie?"

"I-I…" Why the hell hadn't she thought up a good excuse upstairs? "Um. It was uncomfortable, and Zachary…um—a Dom—removed it for me."

"Did he." It wasn't a question, and his eyes didn't leave hers. "Master Zachary?"

"She mouthed off," Zachary said in an unemotional voice. "I removed her corset as a punishment and told her to find you and explain why." Just the facts, damn him.

"Ah." Alex's brows drew together, and his lips flattened. The nervous flutters in Mac's stomach kept moving out until her knees started to tremble.

"You talked back to a Dom. You disobeyed a Dom's direct order. And you disobeyed me. Did I miss anything, MacKensie?" He loomed over her as if he'd added another foot in height.

She tried to swallow. "No, Sir. That's all."

"More than enough, actually. Do you understand what you did wrong?"

This was worse than any chewing out she'd ever had. His eyes held both anger and disappointment. He didn't yell; his voice stayed level.

"Answer me, MacKensie. What did you do wrong?"

"I wasn't polite." She thought about ripping free of his grasp and running, but her feet stayed frozen on the floor. "I didn't obey his order. I didn't wear what you told me to wear." She felt her lip quiver and couldn't stand it. She tried to pull away. "Damn you, I'm not going naked in a roomful of fully dressed people."

She heard gasps from the two other subs.

"Actually, if it pleases me that you be naked, then you will do so and be proud that I choose to share your beauty," he said softly. "In situations like this, what you wear—or don't wear—is at my discretion." He stepped back and crossed his arms over his chest. "Strip. Now."

Her mouth dropped open. "No. No way."

"Well then." Moving so smoothly she didn't realize his intentions, he grasped her wrist, stepped back, and sat on the couch behind him. He pulled her to his right to stand beside his knees. An ironic smile crossed his face. "I think we've done this before."

She stared down at him in confusion. "What?"

He grabbed a handful of her shirtfront and yanked. She landed painfully on her stomach across his knees. "Oomph." Gasping for the air knocked out of her, she struggled to rise.

Her left arm was trapped between their bodies. Alex reached across her back to grip her other arm, holding it against her side and pinning her shoulders at the same time.

"Let me go, dammit!" She tried to roll off his legs.

She felt movement on the backs of her thighs as he pulled her skirt up, baring her bottom. He wouldn't! She fought harder.

Slam!

The shock of his hand striking her bottom rendered her speechless for a second. And then she screamed in fury.

Slam. Slam. Slam. The shocking pain of the stinging blows silenced her.

He said, "I do this because I care for you, MacKensie." His voice sounded almost tender. "I don't like having to punish a sub, but this is for your own good. And because I care."

Slam. Slam. Slam. Each blow stung like a searing flame on her skin.

"Damn you, you asshole. You bastard. I don't—"

Slam. Slam. Slam. She choked as pain began to overwhelm her.

"You were disobedient and disrespectful, as you are now. So you are being punished because I care how you behave." His hand stroked over her burning skin gently, then...

Slam. Slam. Slam.

God, it hurt. Hurt way worse than when he had spanked her before. He was hitting harder. Tears pooled, then ran from her eyes. She tried to free her arm, and his grip tightened to a steel band.

"I can keep this up all night, MacKensie, if that's what it takes to get this through your head. Obedience is rewarded. Respect is rewarded. Subs who disobey are punished."

Slam. Slam. Slam. "If I didn't care about you, I would simply ask you to leave."

She froze as his words entered her, echoing through the hollows inside her. He cared. Cared enough to punish her. He hadn't made her leave.

Slam. Slam. Slam.

A sob welled from deep inside her and wrenched out past her constricted throat. As if the first sob had opened something, the next and next ripped out, faster, hurting her chest.

His hand caressed her bottom, and the pain of his touch mingled with the pleasure of his warmth. "When you apologize and sincerely beg forgiveness, then I will stop."

Never, she'd never. She smothered her sobs. "You bastard," she whispered, yet her defiance lacked real anger.

Slam. Slam. Slam. The blows moved lower to the tender crease of her thigh, the sharp slaps agonizing. She gritted her teeth.

"I was proud of your behavior earlier tonight, of your sweetness and your compassion. You are a beautiful, intelligent woman, MacKensie."

Slam. Slam. Slam.

His words tore through her, more painful than the stinging blows. Something, some dark emotion, tore loose, and her chest shook with its passing. The pain on her skin filled her world even as his words emptied the lake of pain inside her. She couldn't fight either one. He had control.

He cares for me.

"I'm sorry," she whispered. And he held his blow. How could he hear her? But the ringing noise she heard was all inside her head and didn't diminish when he paused.

"That's a start." His hand stroked her back. "Do you know what to do now?"

She remembered from the dungeon a lifetime ago. *"Kneel and apologize."* She nodded.

He released her, and his big hands steadied her as she slid off his legs and onto her knees. Her voice shook as she stared at her hands clenched together in her lap. "I'm sorry, Sir."

No answer.

She looked up. He was waiting for...for the rest. "Please forgive me, Sir." She felt tears still rolling down her cheeks and didn't dare move to wipe them away. His gaze held her pinned as he studied her, looking for...something. She wanted to give him whatever he wanted, and then maybe he'd hold her. She wanted to be held so badly.

"I forgive you, little cat," he said gently. "Strip for me now."

One second of shocked horror and then she caved. He had control, and she'd given it to him. To finish seemed...right, as if it satisfied something within her. Her clothes dropped to the floor, and she stood before him naked.

When he held his arms out, she fell into his embrace.

MacKensie vibrated in his arms like a badly tuned machine; the trembling rolled through her body in waves. Alex tightened his grip, tucking her head into the hollow of his shoulder, and let her feel his warmth and strength. His comfort.

"I'm proud of you, little cat," he murmured, stroking her sweat-damp hair. "It's not easy to submit, even if it's what you want to do. Giving up control takes as much internal strength as taking control. Maybe more."

He glanced up and realized the others had cleared out when the punishment began. Some discipline should be witnessed; some should be private. The Doms had known what he'd planned. They'd helped push MacKensie into defying him so he could give her what she couldn't admit she wanted. From the feel of her in his arms and the calm look on her face when she asked for-giveness, the spanking had satisfied something in her.

His next task would be to find out why.

But first she needed to be held, and he needed to hold her. Erotic pain aside, deliberately hurting a woman could indeed hurt the giver too. A Dom's nature was to *protect* a helpless woman, but sometimes the path to healing came through pain.

He pulled her closer, pleased at the way she snuggled into his arms, as trusting now as a sleepy kitten. And he knew he'd spoken truly a few minutes ago.

He did care.

✦ ✦ ✦ ✦ ✦

A while later, Alex set MacKensie on her feet and picked up two heavy blankets. He wrapped one around her. "Time for some more fresh air."

She glanced toward the clothing still piled on the floor, and he shook his head, amused at her look of outrage. His little cat recovered quickly.

The wind off the Sound moistened his face as he guided her down the beach to a spot where piles of driftwood on three sides gave an illusion of privacy, and the sand hid everything else. Not that restraints would be needed tonight.

After opening his blanket on the sand, he took a seat and used a weather-smoothed log for a backrest. Smiling at her wary expression, he drew MacKensie down to sit between his legs.

She gave a muffled yelp when her sore ass hit the rough blanket, then relaxed, resting her back against his chest, his arms around her waist. It was a rare evening with no rain, and there were few places as lovely as the beach. The waves washed onto shore in a soft rhythm as lighted freighters and ferries traversed the Sound with a slow dignity. Overhead, patchy clouds drifted in front of the waning moon, creating shadows that flowed across the white sand.

Gradually the tension eased from his little sub's body.

"I've canoed on a lake at night," she said, her voice hushed. "This is like it but more...alive."

"Yes." He kissed her cheek. "I'll have to take you to the ocean. Our Sound is sweet and gentle; the Pacific has more moods." In an unhurried move, he slid his hand under the blanket and cupped a pert breast. He could feel as well as hear her sharp inhalation. His arm tightened around her waist, a quiet warning about whose body he held.

He felt the tremor run through her and the stiffening of her muscles. Her discomfort at being touched intimately by a man, even him, hadn't diminished much. He had no intention of pursuing sex now, but he needed his hands on her to read her responses and show him the way.

Most people's beliefs and responses to spanking originated in childhood. He'd start there. "I've lived close to Puget Sound all my life," he said easily. "Where did you grow up, MacKensie?"

"Iowa. You know that," she said. Terse answer. Not a subject she wanted to pursue.

"Ah yes, that's right. Did you grow up in that town you came from? Oak Hollow?" He'd never have detected the quickly controlled jerk if his hand hadn't rested on her breast.

"That's right." She tried to sit up, and he pulled her back.

"Are your parents still there?"

"They died. When I was four."

He felt as if he were Butler, pursuing an elusive mouse through the grass. "Who raised you then?"

"I went into foster care."

She strained against his grip. Foster care might hold the key. "How were you punished in foster care, little cat?"

"Frak, that's not... I'm not going to talk about... None of your business."

Frazzled and a little lost, and the spanking still affected her emotions. He'd counted on that. "Answer me."

"We had time-outs."

Well, that sounded harmless enough, except the tension buzzed through her body so fiercely, it made his hands ache. What could go wrong in a time-out? Length or location? "*Send her where you didn't have to look at her*," she'd said. "Where did you have your time-outs?"

Her whole body stiffened as if he'd hit her.

Right question. "MacKensie?"

"A closet. She'd lock us in a closet," Mac said, her voice thin and high.

"So who got spanked?"

Chapter Twelve

Mac could feel Alex's body surrounding her and his hand on her breast. Yet it was as if the real MacKensie had disappeared, and he held a doll rather than a person. "Her daughter got spanked. Arlene loved her daughter."

"Oh hell," Alex breathed. His words startled her, as did his kiss on her cheek. His scratchy chin nuzzled her neck before he said, "You know, little cat, I could tell you that the old bitch should be shot for abusing children in her care, and that you're a bit confused when it comes to being punished because of her, but my words wouldn't make much difference. Your thinking mind might take it in, but the subconscious resists any change."

Confused? More like totally screwed up. Between her childhood and her whoring days, her internal map of the world looked more like a jigsaw puzzle dropped on the floor. This wasn't a big revelation. And the way her stomach clenched when his hand stroked her breast just emphasized that.

"Did anyone touch you sexually when you were little?" Alex asked. His other hand slid through a gap in the blanket. She gave up holding the edges closed and grabbed his hand. Warm fingers closed on her cold ones.

"MacKensie?"

"No." Her voice came out slightly breathless. "No one."

"Are you going to tell me what happened twelve years ago?"

"No." She tried to pull away again, as useless an effort as a butterfly trying to escape a hungry bird.

"All right." He didn't sound angry, but she knew him now. He didn't give. Persistence should be his middle name. But instead of talking more, he caressed her breast. His fingers circled her nipple, and she could actually feel the tiny muscles in the areola bunching in response to his knowledgeable touch. He moved to the other breast, and as if the two were joined by a wire, they both soon ached.

"Alex, I want to go now. I'm tired."

He pinched her nipple hard enough to make her jerk, and yet the sizzle went straight to her clit. Her pussy started to burn. "Don't lie to me, pet. I prefer a refusal to a lie, but right now, I'll accept neither. I've had a long evening, and I intend to play with my sub a little."

Play with me? A chill crawled up her spine, putting out the heat as if ice water had been dumped on it.

"Yes, play with you," he said, startling her. She hadn't realized she'd spoken. "Don't worry, pet. My cock will stay where it is unless you jump on it. But that's the only concession you get tonight." His fingers tightened on her nipple as if to prove his point. Pressing and then releasing in a slow rhythm until her blood and pussy pulsed in response.

He bit her neck lightly, and she jumped. How did he make all the sensations flow into her clit like water flowing into the ocean? Filling it until it throbbed.

As if he'd heard her, his other hand released her fingers and stroked down her body, ever so gently and yet inexorably. She set her hand over his, lacing her fingers between his and trying to stop him, a useless attempt. When his fingers stroked across her pussy, her fingers were still laced through his.

He chuckled. "I hadn't thought you the type for masturbation in public, but I enjoy watching a woman pleasure herself. You may continue if you want."

She jerked her hand away with a growl, knowing she'd totally lost that round. Heck, she was losing everything, including her senses.

His hand pressed against her pussy, his skin cool against the heat. Then he stroked the wetness from his fingers onto her thigh. "You're wet," he whispered. "I will continue."

How did he do this to her? Men had touched her—many, many men—and rubbed her and—

"Stop thinking," he growled and bit her neck again, totally derailing her thoughts, and then he slid a finger into her.

She jumped, then gasped when his fingers pinched her breast. Her clit felt as if it had been pumped up like a balloon, and a tremor raced through her. Her control eroding like the sand on the beach, she struggled against him. His forearms kept her in place even as his fingers moved over her breast. Her pussy. He swept her moisture through her folds and up over her clit.

And then one finger rubbed her, stroking gently but firmly in a merciless rhythm. He would stop to spread more wetness and then resume. She could actually feel her climax approach this time, feel her legs quivering and her insides winding up like a spring.

He stopped.

Why? She hadn't come.

He tossed the sides of her blanket back, and the cool air swept over her. Apparently he'd gotten bored, she decided, with relief—and disappointment as her clit pulsed with each beat of her heart. "Well, we should go in," she said. She leaned forward, and he yanked her back against his chest so fast, her breath huffed out.

"Stay still, sub."

At his growled command, her body froze, although her heart rate increased.

And then he used his fingers to do exactly the same thing all over again, bringing her right to the top. And stopping.

And again. The next time he stopped, she couldn't smother her moan. He was deliberately torturing her. "Why?"

His hands stroked over her, and everything he did seemed to make her need to come worse. Her clit felt as if it contained all the blood in her body, stabbing with need.

"There's only one way for you to get relief," he murmured. "You're sitting on it."

She realized her bottom pressed against a very erect cock, and she tried to edge away. "No," she whispered. "I won't."

"That's all right, pet," he said. "I enjoy touching you so much that I can keep this up all night." His fingers slid down to cup her pussy, grazing over her clit. Her hips surged up, trying for more, and his hand moved away.

Fine. Surely I can do this myself. She slid her hand down to her pussy.

A ruthless grip closed around her wrist, pulled her hand away. "My toy, not yours," Alex growled.

A minute later he resumed tormenting her, and her arousal surged higher this time, the frustration increasing her need to painful levels.

When he stopped again, she couldn't stand it anymore. She needed...needed so badly to come. Could she actually have sex with him? Alex wasn't a john. Maybe she could let him take her. "All right. Just do it."

"No, little sub." He took his hands off her, and she whimpered. "*You* will do it." He waited.

Her body felt stiff as she turned to face him and knelt between his legs. The swollen folds between her legs throbbed, and the wetness there chilled in the breeze. With shaking fingers, she undid his belt, then his slacks. No underwear. Released, his cock bobbed out, a heavy, thick weapon that men used—

"MacKensie." His hand tilted her head up to meet his gaze. Moonlight fell across his stern jaw. His eyes were dark with shadows but level, not crazy with lust. "Go at your own pace, not mine."

She bit her lip, and his thumb rubbed her chin. He didn't grab her hips and try to shove himself into… His fingers brushed over her clit, and she gasped, fire bursting within her again. She looked at his cock again. "If I put it in, and you get off, then you'll let me finish?"

His eyes narrowed as he studied her face. He sighed and touched a finger to her chin. "Yes, sweetheart. If you put it in, then it will be my pleasure to give you a mind-blowing orgasm."

She shuddered as her pussy clenched. "All right." She could do this. She'd done it so many times before, even if unwilling. But Alex wasn't a john, hadn't given her money, didn't want anything. She moved up to straddle him and eased down until his cock pressed against her opening.

Pushing, ramming, hurting. Her chest tightened until she couldn't breathe. Her ears rang, and she tried to jump off. "Red! Red, red, red—"

Powerful hands closed on her arms. "MacKensie, look at me."

She blinked, then focused on him.

He smiled slightly, and he released her, settling his hands back behind his head. Where they had been when she lost it. His voice held the same gentleness she used with frightened pets. "I'm not touching you, sweetheart. I want you, but at your speed. You can quit anytime."

"Uh." The only one touching anybody was her, and she was definitely touching him—her fingernails were embedded in his shoulders. She pulled her hands away. "Sorry."

"Hang on to me all you want."

She sighed, all too aware of how her pussy hovered above his cock. *Honestly, MacKensie, you gave yourself a panic attack.* He hadn't done a thing. She shook herself mentally. *Frak me, but I'll be damned if I live in fear.*

She gritted her teeth, and—before she could chicken out— she grabbed his cock and slammed herself down on it. "Aaah!" It felt like she'd jammed a boot inside her. Her hands clamped onto his shoulders as she shuddered at the shock.

He chuckled, the bastard, and slid his hands up and down her arms. "Never do things in a half-assed fashion, do you, little sub?"

Her breath slid out and back in as the painful fullness eased. Some. He had a damned big cock. "Now what?" she asked as if she'd never ridden a man's cock before. Her legs quivered when she tried to lift.

"What do you want to do?" he asked as if they were having a conversation, not in the middle of having sex. He didn't yank at her or try to move her. He just lay there, waiting for her. As he'd promised.

"Um."

As she dithered, his hands left her arms to stroke up and down her bare thighs, going a little higher each time, until his thumbs almost grazed her center. Her vagina clenched, and oh, it felt...*awesome.* Having him inside her made every sensation more intense, like using fluorescent markers instead of crayons. She flattened her hands on his chest for balance and lifted up just a fraction. Frak, but the feeling of him sliding inside her was almost as wonderful as when he touched her clit.

She glanced up at him, knowing she must look a sweaty, awful sight, but he was smiling at her in an odd way. Like...like when a child had burst into the office to show off her starred report card and her mother had smiled in just that way. Tender. Proud.

Her breath hitched, and for some strange reason, her eyes burned.

He never moved. Just waited.

She blinked, breathed, gathered her scattered thoughts. Sex. *We're having sex here, MacKensie. Get with the program.* Holding her breath, she daringly rose up farther, then eased back. How could a vagina that had never felt anything before suddenly be so excruciatingly sensitive? Up, down. Her clit throbbed, and everything around his cock started to throb too. Up, down. Faster.

Their joining made squishy sounds, sounds she'd always thought were gross, flesh on flesh. Now even the sounds were exciting. Alex was inside her.

She increased the pace, and her need increased. But nothing quite worked. Her climax seemed just out of reach. She whimpered in frustration. "I don't know how…"

"Let me help, sweetheart." And rather than pounding into her like she had expected, he moved just his hand. His fingers slid to the juncture of their bodies, and the next time she came down, he stroked her pussy. Her whole body went rigid. She groaned and went up and down again, and his finger slid across her clit, pressing against it. The sensations from inside her expanded, joined with those from her clit, and suddenly she screamed as everything, *everything* inside her burst, spasming through her in heart-stopping pleasure so brilliant, the moon faded.

She barely moved, and another wave crashed through her. And another. Her heart had somehow lodged high in her chest, pounding so intensely, it hurt.

Finally she dropped down onto him, a quivering mess, still jerking with the aftershocks. "I… God…" she managed to whisper, feeling as if the world had edged sideways, as if reality itself had changed.

When his arms came around her, she almost cried at the sense of being anchored. He stroked her hair and murmured, "That had to be one of the bravest things I've ever seen, little vet. I'm proud of you."

It came again, that fuzzy feeling inside just from his words and his deep voice. She rubbed her cheek against him. He was proud of her.

So was she, come to think of it. *I had sex. Real sex with a man.*

A few minutes later, a cramp in her legs caught her by surprise. She started to move…and froze. He was still inside her and still completely erect. *What have I done?* She sat up quickly and moaned at the amazing sensation as her weight drove him deeper inside her. "Oh frak, I'm sorry. Sorry. You didn't get off, and I did. I'm sorry."

A long sigh. "MacKensie, much as men don't like to share this fact, we rarely die from not getting off."

"But…"

He looked up at her, a little exasperated, a little amused. Not a trace of anger, although she could feel the way his cock pulsed inside her.

"Don't you want to?" she whispered. He didn't want her? The sense of rejection grayed some of her elation.

Those hard hands closed on her arms again. "Little sub, I would be more than delighted to roll you over and take you, here and now. But not if you aren't ready."

She frowned. He'd been inside her for…for a long time. Her johns had usually erupted within minutes, if not seconds. "Couldn't you…? Why didn't you…come before? Before I did?"

He chuckled. "That would defeat the purpose, now wouldn't it? And I didn't want anything to divert you. Little cat, don't worry a—"

"Then take me," she said recklessly. So many others had. How could she deny this one person who actually cared about her? Who'd given her a real, actual orgasm. Her insides still quivered. "However you want."

He cupped her cheek. "Sugar, I… You do realize that I would have to move to get off?"

Do I realize? If he only knew. The laugh that rose into her chest felt almost hysterical, and she smothered it. *Grunting and sloppy, heaving and pushing, battering at her…* Her hands tightened on his shirt. "I realize. Do it."

He studied her again, and she tried to hide how her mind kept screaming, No no no. "All right, then," he said. "I think perhaps we'd best get this behind us, or you'll keep worrying about it." His hands rubbed her legs, and she could feel the way her muscles shook. "I would have preferred you on top"—when he grinned, the lack of lust in his face, the humor in his eyes, relieved her immensely—"but your legs aren't going to hold you up, are they?"

And just like that, he pushed her off him, his cock leaving her body, leaving her empty. "Uhhh." The sound was almost a whine and had come from her. But she didn't have time to think before he'd slid her down onto the blanket and on her back. Such a vulnerable position, she realized as he loomed over her. Her hands fisted.

I can do this. No retreat, no surrender.

Chapter Thirteen

He hadn't planned to go this far yet, but she'd mustered her courage, and to throw her gesture away would be wrong. Alex frowned at how her little hands had fisted. Perhaps a diversion would give her something else to concentrate on. Her fear of men appeared separate from her enjoyment of being dominated. "MacKensie, give me your wrists."

With a quizzical look, she complied. He pulled the Velcro cuffs from under the log, shook the sand off, and fastened them to her wrists.

"Alex?" She moved her arms. Her eyes widened when the chains attached to the cuffs erupted from the sand.

Smiling, he grasped her waist and slid her down the blanket until the chains pulled her arms over her head.

"I didn't say you could do this," she said, her voice shaking.

"Little sub, I didn't ask." When he attached cuffs to her ankles and took up the slack in the chains running to the stakes hidden in the sand, she watched him with big eyes. He ran a finger under each of the cuffs to ensure her circulation wasn't compromised, then sat back on his heels and enjoyed the sight of his restrained submissive.

Her pale, pale skin glowed in the moonlight. Her breasts sat high on her chest, nipples jutting upward, reassuring him that the restraints had given her more arousal than fear. The curly hair between her legs glistened in the light, and when he set his hand there, her quick inhalation was louder than the sound of the waves. He slid his fingers along her folds, circled her clit, and watched the flush rise in her cheeks. Her pussy had softened after her orgasm, but as he continued, the little nub under his fingers swelled with blood. He'd learned from their playtime at the club that she had a sensitive clit, and stroking the sides worked better than on top.

Playing with the very edge of the hood could make her whine. Hearing that sound again… *Hell.* Unable to resist, he went down on her. A woman with her legs chained open presented an overwhelming temptation to get closer, to breathe in the scent of her arousal, to taste her juices. And torture her until she whimpered.

He laid his tongue directly on that tender clit and heard the thin whine rise higher. He flicked the edges, did a few circles, and then gently pulled her labia apart and the hood up. The *pearl of sensation*—damned good term.

Her legs shook when the cool air hit the protected nub, and he could feel her muscles tense. He flicked the edges of the button ever so lightly until her breathing turned ragged.

He could get her off again. No, he had better not push her further. She'd wanted to gift him with herself, and if she panicked now, it would be a step back. Besides, he very much wanted to bury himself deep inside her. He sat up, enjoying her frustrated whimper. Her climax was just a flick or two away.

Watching her face, he positioned himself and pressed in, a hell of a lot slower than she'd done it. Her pussy, hot and wet, stretched around him as he filled her.

If her fear hadn't hit, she'd have climaxed with his entry. But they had time. He propped himself up with one arm and took her lips in a teasing kiss. Her eyes looked a little wild, so he reminded her she had other worries than his cock. "Did I get the chains too tight?"

Her breath caught, and she jerked her arms, her legs. She was well pinned, and he could feel the way her pussy constricted around him at the knowledge. The purely submissive response fed his Dom nature like raw meat tossed to a wolf.

"You know, I like your legs tied open, little sub; I can lick you, and you can't stop me." Her vagina gave an involuntary twitch, but her eyes still had terror lurking in the back.

He slid his hand under her ass. "Maybe next time I spank you, I'll tie you down first." He squeezed the tender skin where his hand had struck. Her hips jolted up, pushing him deeper inside her, and her moan of pain held the husky note of arousal. This time, when he looked into her eyes, no terror showed.

Now she was ready. Smiling, he pulled back and then drove into her. Her instinctive reaction—fear—made her yank on the restraints, and as that diverted her, he rocked in and out, harder and faster.

She felt like the finest of dreams, enclosing his cock in hot satin, smooth and slick. Too damn good. Now that he'd released the control he'd kept over his need, he wouldn't last long. Damned if he wouldn't make her go over with him. Abandoning her ass, he ran his hands over her breasts, reminding her she had other sensitive body parts. Each pinch on a nipple made her pussy contract. He wet his fingers, sliding them over her clit until it stiffened.

Capturing it between thumb and index finger, he rubbed, then pinched it gently with each of his strokes.

"Not again," she whimpered.

He felt her body shift from the "this is fun and exciting" into the "God, I need to come" stage, and her hips rocked against his as she tried to hurry his thrusts, push against his fingers.

She squeezed around him, thigh and stomach muscles quivering. She was right on the edge. He shifted to the hard, fast strokes that would take him with her, angling to hit her G-spot with every couple of thrusts. When he slid a finger directly over her clit and rubbed, her whole body went rigid.

One thrust, another, and then her head tilted back, neck cords standing out as her climax burst over her. Her short, jerky cries coincided with the forceful, milking convulsions that sucked his cock like a vacuum pump and then yanked him right over the top. His climax started at his feet, squeezed his balls like a vise, and finally erupted from his cock in such brutal spasms that his eyes went blind.

His arms almost buckled as he blinked and shook his head experimentally—no, it hadn't exploded. He looked down at the little sub underneath him.

Her eyes were glazed.

"Little cat," he murmured, resting his forehead against hers. Just that tiny movement tightened her pussy around him, and he actually jerked a couple more times. This woman could be the death of him.

Reaching over her head, he ripped the Velcro cuffs off and released her wrists. She lowered her hands, hesitated, and then wrapped her arms around him. *Good.* Propping himself up with one hand, he nuzzled her neck, then kissed her long and deep as he stroked her face, her breasts, her waist. Women needed closeness after sex—any man soon learned that—and this little sub would need it more than most.

Not that he considered having his hands on her any hardship. The need to touch her and keep her close was stronger than he'd felt with any woman. "Thank you, sweetheart," he murmured. "You have a generous heart."

"I think I owe the thanks," she whispered, and he could hear the quiver in her voice. "You got me off…twice. Even though this last time was supposed to be just for you."

He snorted. "Little sub, you have a lot to learn about sex." And she needed more holding than this position allowed. "Brace yourself," he warned and smiled at her confused look until he pulled out of her. At the loss of his cock, she mewed in unhappiness, pleasing him immensely.

After releasing her legs, he lay down beside her and pulled her up against him. Her head fit into the hollow of his shoulder as if designed for that purpose. He kept her pinned against him with one arm and let his other hand roam over the muscles of her back, the sweet place where her waist curved in, the tiny dents just above her buttocks, the perfect curve of her ass.

A wiggle and whimper reminded him of the tenderness of that ass, probably still reddened from his hand.

He chuckled. "Sorry. I forgot." The growl she gave in response sounded like a kitten wanting to be a tiger and proved the final straw for him.

This one, here in his arms—she was a keeper.

✧ ✧ ✧ ✧ ✧

Mac had achieved an orgasm with a man inside her. Just like a normal woman. She stared into the blackness of the beach-house bedroom and just marveled. However this change in her had happened, she liked it. Liked it a lot. Why Alex could get past her defenses when no one else had, she didn't know.

Was it because he'd spanked her...twice now? She had to admit that she felt...accepted by him, even with all her weirdnesses. She smiled in the darkness; he surrounded her even in sleep. He'd curled his big body around her, pulling her shoulders against his chest. Her head rested on his right arm. His other arm held her against him. His hand cupped around her breast.

She should find the position terrifying and his hand too intimate, but she didn't. It felt comforting. Not that he'd given her a choice. He'd simply lain down beside her, rolled her over, and yanked her into his arms.

He'd done that all evening, hadn't he? *Dominated* her; oh, that was definitely the word. Including that spanking. As she'd thought about the evening, she'd realized that he'd planned the whole thing. The other Doms had deliberately pushed her into disobeying him, and she'd fallen right into his trap.

She could still feel his hand slamming down on her bare bottom and hear his deep voice reassuring her at the same time. "*I care about you...*" She shivered. How could the memory of a man hitting her make her want to crawl deeper into his arms?

But he'd known that too, considering how he'd held her after the spanking. And on the beach after they'd had sex, he'd held her for a very, very long time, as if he knew she needed that reassurance. How could he read her so easily? The knowledge that he could made a little shiver creep up her spine.

But I got off. Damn, he could know her as well as he wanted if she could do that again. Just thinking about sex with him... How funny that even thinking about his hand—about his finger—touching her so intimately, rubbing her clit... Just *thinking* about it made heat wash through her. And with him inside? That had been like nothing—*nothing*—she'd ever felt before.

Why was she stewing about this anyway? Dawn arrived in another hour, and there were guests here, and...she was wide awake. She should never have let her mind dwell on sex with Alex. She could feel how wet she'd gotten. Heaven help her.

She heard a chuckle, and then Alex's hand squeezed her breast, making her gasp. He slid his hand down between her legs to the betraying wetness.

"I've created a monster," he murmured and bit the back of her neck. The unexpected sharpness sent a sizzle straight to her pussy, and she jolted.

His tongue laved the tiny hurt. "I'm too lazy to move right now, but no matter." His hips slid down a little ways, and when he moved back up, his cock pressed against her. He slid the arm underneath her down until his hand gripped her hip, securing her in place as his thick cock pushed into her.

She stiffened against the unexpected burning pain of his entry.

He made a sympathetic noise, but both hands held her hips securely against his groin, not letting her move away. She could hear the amusement in his voice when he said, "After twelve years without, you might be a bit sore."

"You sadist," she hissed, ignoring the way his possessive hands made her body thrill.

He laughed. "Oh, not really. When we go to the club next, I'll show you the difference." He moved inside her, and the pain disappeared under a wave of pleasure. And then he moved one hand to slide over her clit. If she'd thought her pussy was swollen before, she was so, so wrong. She could actually feel her clit engorge and stiffen under his skillful fingers.

He began to thrust, using one hand on her clit to drive her mad and the other to anchor her so securely, she could only take it. *Be taken.* And the pleasure built into a frenzy, shocking her when it broke over her in an overwhelming orgasm. Her hips bucked uncontrollably against the restraining hands. "God."

He moved his hand off her pussy and nuzzled her neck before murmuring, "That was too fast and easy, little sub. I'm going to want you to come again and much longer. I'll give you…oh, a minute to recover."

She whimpered.

✧   ✧   ✧   ✧

Mac had come the second time as demanded—not that he'd accept anything less—and then again when he walked right into her shower. He soaped her down, shoved her legs apart, and licked her into a knee-buckling orgasm before pushing her against the wall to take his own pleasure. When his tongue stroked into her mouth in the same rhythm as his thrusts, she felt invaded, top and bottom. And came again.

Afterward he'd dressed and gone downstairs while she knelt by the suitcase, trying to decide what to wear. The sadistic jerk had slapped her butt on the way out of the room, reminding her how sore parts of her anatomy still felt. In fact, she had a lot of tender places today. Breasts and mouth and private parts and bottom. Muscles in her legs and stomach that hadn't worked out like that in years. If ever.

She dressed, still smiling, and walked through the kitchen door into the midst of the entire group.

"Perhaps if we—" Leaning against the counter, Alex broke off his conversation with Peter to watch his little sub walk into the kitchen. Her mouth was swollen, her cheeks beard burned, and her big brown eyes held a languid glow. She'd chosen to wear jeans and a blue T-shirt with a pile of kittens displayed on the front. Barefoot and tousled and sexy as hell.

His cock hardened, which should be an impossibility considering he'd just fucked them both silly in the shower. He grinned, remembering how her legs had buckled when he released her.

She smiled at the subs seated at the table and the Doms at the stove, and then her cheeks flushed. Probably remembering last night and how they'd seen her bare assed and being spanked. "Good morning." Her voice had the huskiness of a woman well used.

Beside Alex, Peter nodded to her. "Good morning, MacKensie. Bacon's on the stove; eggs are on the table."

She nodded and walked to the stove. After giving Alex a quick glance, she averted her gaze and reached for the pan.

Alex frowned. He didn't like how she placed herself at a distance rather than within his personal space. It showed her insecurities when it came to male-female relationships. He rubbed his jaw and considered. She'd been sixteen the last time she had sex; had she even attempted a relationship since? What the *hell* had happened to her back then?

Something to work on later. Right now... Well, each relationship ran on a different track, but he could show her how theirs would go, and it didn't include acting indifferent to each other in public.

When he tucked a finger into the waistband of her jeans and pulled her between his outstretched legs, she gave him a startled look. Ignoring the stiffness of her body, he lifted her up against him far enough that he could enjoy her lips. He dallied, taking pleasure in the lingering taste of mint toothpaste as he coaxed her into responding. Slowly her muscles released the tension until she sagged against him, and then her body filled with a different kind of tension.

When he set her back on her feet, her face was flushed, her breathing fast, and the uncertainty was definitely gone. She shook her head at him, giving him a look that held both exasperation and delight. And when she reached for a plate, her hip rubbed against his.

Much better.

Chapter Fourteen

A few days later, Mac stopped just inside the door of Alex's office. "I made some stir-fry if you want some."

Seated at his desk, Alex didn't move. She walked into the office and stopped behind him, enjoying the scent of leather and books and his subtle aftershave. "Alex?"

He looked up and blinked, and then his eyes focused, the blue intensifying. He took her hand. "MacKensie. I'm sorry. Were you speaking to me?"

She laughed. "Breaking your concentration is like hitting a brick wall with a pencil. Can't even dent it."

"Sorry, sweetheart." He pushed the chair back and pulled her into his lap. One thorough kiss later, he asked, "Now, what can I help you with?"

Would she ever get used to him? He never asked, *What have you done for me?* It was always, *What can I do for you?*

"What are you working on?" She stalled to give her body time to settle down. Damn him, he'd sure grabbed her a lot over the past few days, and this morning, she'd realized his purpose: to make her give up her instinctive flinching away from men. He'd seize her, then follow the sudden move with the comfort of a kiss or hug, but nothing else.

No, when he wanted sex, he didn't grab, he moved on her smooth and slow and... She bit her lip against the onrush of warmth.

His eyes narrowed, and he murmured, "Now that must have been an interesting thought."

"Well..." She grinned. The stir-fry could keep, right? But then her stomach rumbled.

Before she could think, he set her on her feet and rose. "Time for a little vet to eat." He cupped her cheek with one big hand and ran his thumb over her lips, making her crave the feel of his lips over hers. "We can play later."

When he took her hand to lead her out of the room, she shook her head with a sigh of exasperation. Did he give off some sort of pheromone that made her thoughts go immediately to sex? It seemed like whenever she touched him, her head entered some sort of sexual fog.

"I made stir-fry. That's what I came to tell you," she told him as they left the office. "What were you working on that had you so oblivious?"

"A senior-services company. They send aides to help elderly people with medications or getting dressed or shopping, whatever they need. They're trying to figure out whether expanding would be worth their while."

"And they asked you?" As they entered the kitchen, the smell of food made her stomach gurgle again. She'd forgotten to grab lunch. "I thought you just gave little companies money so they could get started."

"No." He took plates from the cupboard. "We tried, but too many went belly-up. Having great ideas doesn't guarantee having business sense. Now when we stake a start-up, they get me or another consultant as part of the package. Since we started the hands-on approach, the failure rate has dropped by half."

"Makes sense." She poured them each a glass of wine and followed him to the windowed breakfast nook where they took most of their meals. She loved this room. The Sound never looked the same, and when the massive Olympic Mountains peeked out from their cloud cover, they took her breath away. "When the new guy bought Jim's vet clinic, he made quite a few mistakes that either Jim or I could have warned him about if we'd known." Come to think of it, she needed to call Brent. He owed her one last check, and she'd need it to pay the utility bill.

Lights across the water flickered on as twilight settled in. Tail wagging, Butler trotted in from the backyard, never one to miss a chance at tidbits from the table.

Alex took a bite of stir-fry, and his eyebrows rose. "This is excellent."

His compliment created a warm glow inside her. The housekeeper came in every other day to clean and always left something in the refrigerator to heat up for supper—and wasn't that so cool?—but Mac enjoyed creating meals, especially here, where fresh fish and vegetables abounded. And she did make a hell of a stir-fry, if she said so herself.

"Who is Jim?" Alex asked.

"He owned the vet clinic where I worked." *He saved me, loved me like a daughter, taught me how honest and caring some men could be.* She swallowed. "When he died, I had nothing to keep me in Oak Hollow." Except his house, and that would go up for sale as soon as she had somewhere else to live.

Alex studied her for a second. "That's why you're relocating?"

"Pretty much." Emptiness welled up inside her as she remembered the aching loneliness after Jim's death. But being with Alex had lightened the desolation, at least for now. She needed to remember what he'd said—that he didn't want a girlfriend, just the appearance of one—and not let herself get used to being with him. Her eyes burned suddenly, and she slid off her chair to pet Butler until the need to cry had passed.

When she returned to the table, she saw the curiosity in Alex's eyes. But anything she told him about Jim and Mary would open the way to more questions, and Alex would find out about her past. She couldn't bear to see the disgust on his face. The past needed to stay in the past. "I—"

"What made you pick Seattle?"

She blinked at the unexpected question. "Uh, I...I heard some people talking about it once." At a vet convention. Mac had waited in a corner while Ajax rounded up business, and she'd overheard some Seattleites talking about home. It had been her last night as a whore; maybe that's why she'd remembered their conversation so well: "*Lakes and mountains and the ocean. I didn't want anywhere dry and brown, and I didn't want to shovel snow anymore.*"

Alex grinned at her mock shiver.

"I wanted to try a city." *Big enough to get lost in. As far away from Iowa as possible, without drowning in the Pacific.* She smiled at Alex. "So...you want to watch a movie tonight, or are you returning to work?"

"A movie." A corner of his mouth curved up. "Since it's my turn to decide, we'll watch *Patton*. Or possibly *The Thin Red Line*."

"Frak that. It's not your—"

"I keep forgetting to ask," he interrupted. "What is *frak*?"

Could anyone have lived in this century and not seen *Battlestar Galactica*? Really? She eyed him uneasily. Maybe he was really an alien, here to take over the world and—

"MacKensie, pay attention. Frak?"

"Uh, right. From *Battlestar Galactica*, the new one. They used it in place of...uh...*fuck*."

"Ah." His finger rubbed his lips, and she could see him smothering a smile, undoubtedly because of her red face.

Considering all the times he'd...fucked...her, why should the word be so hard to say? She frowned at him. "Anyway, it was a TV series. And when it came out on DVD, Jim and I watched it again." She smiled at the memory. "God, I love that show."

"I'll add it to the library, then."

She jerked her gaze back to him. "You will not."

"Excuse me?"

"You don't like science fiction, so you'd be buying it for me. And you're not going to do that."

One eyebrow tilted up. "I'm not?"

"No." Maybe she was being rude, but still...

"Do you not like presents, little cat?" he asked softly.

"I—" She pushed back from the table and stepped around Butler to walk across the room and back. "You see, presents are— should be reciprocal in a way. But I don't have any money, so I can't give you anything back, and just taking things makes me feel"— *like a whore*—"useless. And greedy."

He had that observant look in his eyes again, that stillness in his body that showed he'd focused totally on her. But then he smiled and said gently, "All right, sweetheart. I can see how you might feel that way." He held his hand out to her, one of those silent commands that tilted her world.

How did he do this to her? Even when he wasn't being a Dom, he was. She put her hand in his.

And then he grinned. "So since we don't have any good science fiction, we're watching *Patton* tonight."

"We are not." Their ongoing fight. Chick flicks and science fiction versus his war movies. Actually, she loved having someone with whom to watch a movie, even if the movie sucked. Not just watch either. Since their time at the beach, the movies had acquired "intermissions." He'd taken her in front of the fireplace, bent over the arm of a couch, and while straddling his legs on the chair. If she gave him any trouble—or if the mood struck him— she might find her hands bound.

Or ordered to stay in one place without moving. God, that had been so difficult—lying on her back, legs open, hands over her head while he... She swallowed and caught the simmer of heat in his eyes.

"I want to see *Sleepless in Seattle*. It seems only appropriate considering I'm living here," she said, ignoring the way her voice had turned husky. "We'll flip for it." She pulled away and carried her dishes out to the kitchen.

Alex set his dishes beside hers on the counter. Then firm hands closed around her waist, and he set her on the kitchen island.

"Hey." She frowned at him. "What—"

Clever fingers unbuttoned her shirt. "I want dessert before my movie."

She'd fallen asleep, curled in his lap, head on his shoulder. He kissed the top of her head, enjoying the light citrus fragrance of her hair and the heavier scent of hot, raunchy sex. The movie she'd chosen continued to play, but he'd muted the sound when she drifted off.

Interviewing for jobs must be hard work. Probably living with him was harder.

She'd come a long way in the past week. She didn't flinch away from his touch now, and her responses during sex were uninhibited and responsive. God, he enjoyed making love to her.

But holding her like this, teasing her during their meals, waking with her in his arms, pleased him just as much. In fact, he couldn't envision the house without her in it. Butler made good company, and listened attentively to Alex's complaints about idiotic managers, but he couldn't come up with suggestions as MacKensie did. Or laugh when Alex told of the latest fiasco. As a dining companion, Butler left something to be desired too.

He shook his head slightly. What the hell was he thinking? He didn't want a relationship, dammit. He liked his life, his solitude, and having his house to himself. Or he had.

His little sub wouldn't be leaving right away, though. He'd talked her into staying at least a couple of more weeks, or until she secured a position. Her reluctance had bothered him, until he realized it had nothing to do with him but originated in her hatred of being under obligation to someone. To anyone.

She certainly had an abundance of pride. In many ways, she reminded him of his mother, and wasn't that an appalling thought?

Mac stirred and murmured, and he realized she'd stiffened. Her head thrashed back and forth, and the high whimpers she gave sounded like those of a child. Her hands opened and closed.

"MacKensie, wake up," he said, keeping his voice low. Non-threatening. "Wake up now."

Her eyes opened. She blinked up at him, then looked around the room. "Not a closet," she whispered.

"No closet," he agreed. He stroked her shoulder.

"I hate locked doors, you know," she confided, still muzzy with sleep. "I have to open them."

"Do you now?" And there, in two little sentences, she'd given him the answer to his unlocked dungeon. "How did you learn to do that?"

"Jenny taught me. She was a lot older, at least thirteen, and her dad taught her to pick locks. That's why they put her in foster care. She carried her picks everywhere. I do too. I can open almost anything." Eyes half closed, his little sub smiled up at him sweetly.

His little master of locked doors. Huffing a laugh, Alex ran a hand down her arm, and she settled, sighing softly. Her body trusted him instinctively, or she'd never allow herself to sleep in his arms, but her subconscious, holder of all her secrets?

He'd made progress. But he wanted more. He wanted the rest of her story, the reason she'd not had sex for twelve years, the reason she stiffened whenever a man touched her unexpectedly. Rape... He'd thought rape at first, but it didn't quite fit. Her attitude toward sex hadn't been fear as much as revulsion and coldness at the thought of being intimate. Her emotions would shunt away to somewhere else. No, he didn't see violence during sex in her past…but perhaps abuse?

Pulling her closer, he rubbed his cheek against her silky, golden hair. Somehow he needed to get her to talk. As her lover, he wanted to know; as her Dom, he needed to know. But for tonight, he'd take the little confidence she'd just shared with him.

Mac eyed her evening gown, which she needed to somehow don without ripping off her fancy nails or messing up her hair. She held out her hand and grinned at the sparkling colors of her perfectly rounded fingernails. *Amazing.*

Earlier in the day, Hope had arrived and dragged Mac right out of the house. *"The guys are treating us,"* she'd said, obviously delighted to have company at the ritzy spa she took Mac to.

Sadly inexperienced in all the girl rituals, Mac had thought she'd have been intimidated by the staff and have a terrible time. But with Hope chattering away, the afternoon went quickly as they giggled and indulged in facials, soaks, scrubs, and massages. Now Mac ran her hand over her arm. Her skin had never felt so smooth and soft.

Other places were smooth also, and hadn't that just been fun? No one had told Mac all of what Alex had ordered and paid for. Like the horrendous thing called *waxing*, where they'd ripped the hair right off her legs. Frak, that hurt…but then they'd moved higher. *Oh. My. God.* Well, her pussy was now bare and smooth.

And she planned to kill Alex dead when she got the chance.

After a glass of wine, she'd managed to stop whimpering as she and Hope went on to get their hair styled, manicures, pedicures—someone had even done her makeup.

And now…with infinite care, she put on her gown. As she pulled the straps up over her arms, she glanced in the mirror and stared. God, she looked…fantastic. Elegant. The beautician had French braided her hair in a deceptively simple style, weaving in tiny strands of diamond-laced pink ribbon that matched Mac's gown. *I sparkle.*

"Very nice." Alex appeared in the mirror behind her and zipped up the back of the gown. Or maybe it should be called the butt of the dress, considering the absence of any material from her shoulders to her hips. She jumped when Alex's hand slid down her spine and stopped just above her bottom. On bare skin. "Dancing with you will be a pleasure," he murmured. Moving closer, he bent his head and kissed her in the hollow below her ear, making a humming sound when he smelled the exotic perfume one of the women had insisted was her fragrance.

His approval made her glow more than all the pampering. She glanced in the mirror again and smiled. Of course, she did look nice. Really, really nice. And he'd arranged it all.

All. She raised her chin, scowling into Alex's eyes in the mirror. "You sadist," she snapped. "You told them to…" She felt her face turning red and sputtered out, "Do you know how much that hurts?"

Her move away from him was forestalled when he put one unyielding arm around her waist. His other hand slid down her gown to press against her groin. The feel of silky fabric, then the warmth of his hand penetrating to her poor bare pussy made her shiver, and he chuckled.

"I'll make amends later," he murmured in her ear, and she could feel his cock hardening where he pressed against her from behind.

She thought about what his mouth would feel like on all that newly bare, sensitive skin, and her breathing hitched. "Mmmmh."

She cleared her throat against the constriction. "You do that, then."

"Oh I intend to." With a low laugh, he nipped the top of her shoulder, and her nipples puckered so tightly, they ached.

She pulled in a breath. Enough, or they'd spend the evening in bed. She moved far enough away to turn. Getting a good look at him, she blinked. "Wow. You clean up pretty nice, Mr. Fontaine."

His eyes crinkled, only adding to the devastating effect of all that masculinity in a black tuxedo. "Thank you. Now you may tell Butler the same." He nodded at the door.

She followed his gaze and burst out laughing. Sitting politely by the door, Butler had on a dog-style tux and bow tie. Rather than appearing chagrined by the costume, he looked quite proud of himself.

"You look stunning, Butler. I'm going to be with the two most gorgeous males there tonight."

Butler's muzzle rose a little in acknowledgment of this truth.

Well, the evening couldn't be all bad if people brought their pets. She took a deep breath as Alex draped her cape over her shoulders.

Now if she only didn't do anything stupid…

Chapter Fifteen

T he black-tie event of the fall, one newspaper had called it. Mac gaped like a hick as they walked through a hotel lobby filled with the elite of Seattle society, many of whom had pet escorts ranging from Chihuahuas in chiffon tutus to Great Danes in diamond-studded collars.

One German shepherd paraded around in a crown and kingly robes. "Oh my, just look at him." After a second, Mac recalled herself. "Butler, you're the best-looking dog here."

Butler gave her a dignified tail wave in answer.

Holding Butler's leash, Alex chuckled. "The pet stores do a brisk business before the ball." He set his hand on her lower back, and his thumb stroked over her bare skin.

Giving him an exasperated look, she saw the amusement in his eyes. He definitely liked her backless gown. As he guided her through the crowd, exchanging greetings with people here and there, Mac tried not to enjoy the protective feeling of his arm around her. *Don't get used to it, MacKensie. Nothing like this lasts.*

Although she wouldn't lose him for at least two more weeks.

Really, she shouldn't have let him talk her into staying, but her common sense and her own desire had overcome her pride. But once she had a job, then her common sense would be satisfied, and she'd leave.

Frak, I'll miss him.

When the hotel manager cornered Alex with questions about the auction, Mac watched the people milling around and realized she didn't know any of them. *Good.* No one to point fingers or whisper behind her back. And yet loneliness created a little hollow in her chest. After the hotel manager bustled away, she asked, "Will Hope and Peter be here?"

Alex brushed his knuckles over her cheek, his look so tender, she couldn't move. "We'll find them in the auction area. Peter volunteered to oversee one of the tables."

They made it at least twenty feet before they were stopped again. Alex performed introductions, talked briefly, and moved on. Ten feet. Introductions. Chatting as Butler politely exchanged sniffs with each leashed pet. Ten more feet. "Do you know everyone here?" Mac finally asked.

"Fontaine Industries owns various businesses, properties, and all that, so I know a lot of people, yes. And those who support the dog and cat programs come every year." He grinned and bent down to pat Butler. "This is Butler's fourth year."

"Alex, good to see you." A middle-aged brunette in a scarlet gown strolled over. "The auction is a hit. How did you finagle those cruise-ship packages?"

"I have a sweet-talking manager who I sicced on the cruise lines." Alex smiled at Mac. "Susan, this is my friend MacKensie Taylor. She's a vet from the Midwest and plans to relocate here to Seattle. Mac, this is Susan Weston. She runs the Weston Animal Hospital."

They talked briefly about Mac's first view of the Sound and mountains, then the work Susan did for the spay-neuter programs. By the time Susan excused herself, Mac had decided to add Susan's hospital to her list of places to apply.

As they drifted toward the huge room set up for the silent auction, Mac met ten more veterinarians, most of whom owned their own clinics. "Don't any middle-class people attend this event?" she asked finally when she and Alex were alone.

"Not too many," he said absently, nodding at a couple. "It's four hundred dollars a plate."

She stopped dead, and he'd taken two steps past her before realizing she was gone. With a huffed laugh, he returned. Running his hands up and down her bare arms, he said, "Relax, pet. Keeping the price high draws the big spenders so we can soak them good in the auction room. That is the point, after all."

"Yes, but—"

"Just treat everyone like Butler does," he advised. "His only concern is if a person smells good and knows how to pet a dog properly."

Hearing his name, Butler looked up and wagged his tail.

Mac pulled in a breath. "Okay. I...sorry. I just hadn't realized—thought about..." She shrugged helplessly. God, she was so far out of her class... Her chest ached.

Alex's hands tightened on her arms. "No. I don't want to see that look in your eyes." He frowned at her. "People are people. A lot of the ones here inherited money. They didn't do anything productive to earn it. Others gave up everything to get rich. Does having money and no character make a person admirable?"

But if they knew what she'd done? *But they don't, stupid. Get over it.* She looked great, and the most gorgeous man in the place escorted her. Her lips curved. "All right. Sorry. Momentary panic attack," she said lightly.

Alex kissed her cheek gently. "Now that's character," he said, then continued leading her into the auction room.

"MacKensie!"

Mac froze, then grinned as a tiny streak of electric blue sped across the room. "Hope, you're here."

"Look at you! You look awesome." Hope clapped her hands, then wrinkled her nose at Alex. "Phht, you don't deserve her, you know."

Mac's mouth dropped open. When Peter appeared and drew Alex's attention, she edged closer to Hope and whispered, "Won't you get in trouble talking to him that way?"

Hope giggled. "No. The rules are for play or... Well, each couple is different. Some are truly Master and slave all the time, but those in our little group aren't." She shook her head. "Of course, if I give him too much grief, he'll make me suffer for it the next time we all get together."

When Peter and Hope headed back to their station at an auction table, an older woman broke away from a small group. Wearing a silvery gown that accented her blue eyes and silver hair, she seemed the epitome of dignity. Taking Alex's hand, she kissed his cheek lightly and said, "I'm giving a dinner party next Friday, and I'd like you to attend."

Mac frowned at how familiar her voice sounded. Maybe from one of the vet's offices or...

"Why don't you bring Cynthia with you?" the woman asked.

Do not glare; glaring is not polite. Mac smoothed her expression out with an effort. But maybe this was a good time to go hang out with Peter and Hope for a bit. She started to edge away.

Alex's hand wrapped around her arm, holding her in place. "Cynthia moved to Rome, Mother."

Rome? *Mother? Oh frak.* She didn't think she moved, but the fingers around her arm tightened.

"Mother, I'd like you to meet my friend MacKensie Taylor, who is moving here from the Midwest. MacKensie, this is my mother, Victoria Fontaine."

"Pleased to meet you," Mac said, forcing sincerity into her voice.

"Welcome to Seattle, Miss Taylor," Victoria said with not a speck of warmth. "If you'll excuse me, I want to check our seating arrangements." She tilted her head at her son, patted Butler, nodded to Mac, and swept away.

How long did you have to be rich before you learned to walk like a queen? Mac wondered, shoving aside the pain from being so obviously detested. She glanced at Alex. "I didn't realize you have family here." Actually, since she wasn't used to having any, she hadn't even thought about it.

"Please forgive my mother," Alex said softly. "My father was unfaithful and had a liking for blondes, so Mother acts as if every pretty blonde is a hooker."

A hooker. Mac felt the blood slide right out of her face, and her hands clenched. "Nothing to forgive," she said hastily. "But I just spotted the ladies' room. If you and Butler will excuse me, please?" Before he could grab her and quiz her, she escaped. She knew her hasty retreat not only didn't look like a queen's but displayed no dignity whatsoever.

Decorated in floral wallpaper with blue tiling the color of Alex's eyes, the elegant powder room held several brocade-covered chairs. Her legs none too steady, Mac sank into one gratefully. Alex's mother thought blondes were hookers. If she only knew... Mac gave a short laugh and buried her face in her hands.

After a minute, her brain clicked back on. *Overreacting here.*

Really now, although Alex made her feel wonderful and she really liked him, he wasn't...wasn't... She stared at her hands, watching the sparkles on her fingernails. Well, yes, he *was*. She'd fallen for him in a big way. But they had a deal, and he'd made it very, very clear right from the beginning that he didn't want a real girlfriend. *Temporary, Mac, try to remember that.*

So fine. On a more positive note, that meant whatever his mother thought of MacKensie wasn't important at all. Besides, she lived in Seattle now, not Oak Hollow; no one knew her past...mistakes.

Mac raised her chin and straightened her spine. Alex had brought her here to help her find a job. She'd better get with the program.

✧ ✧ ✧ ✧ ✧

An hour later, the most tedious part of the evening—speeches and acknowledgments and awards—had concluded, the program deliberately kept short and sweet.

Since Alex found sit-down meals at an event this size far from palatable, two years ago he'd prevailed and hors d'oeuvres were served buffet-style instead. Each of the many long tables along the wall featured the artistry of a different local chef, and after serving themselves, guests could sit and eat or wander around.

Alex had seen to the feeding of his little sub, although she had no appetite, especially when she realized they had to sit in the front of the room. A glass of wine helped her color. After the speeches were done, he took her table-hopping, choosing vet contacts she'd find useful and people he thought she'd enjoy. His friends tended to be good, down-to-earth people. He'd enjoyed watching as she charmed the pets at each table and then their owners. God knew she charmed the hell out of him.

With a sense of anticipation, he had introduced her to his uncle. An excellent judge of character, Uncle Andrew had disliked Cynthia within minutes of meeting her. He obviously fell for MacKensie just as quickly and was now trying to talk her into joining the family for a day sail through the San Juan Islands.

Alex lost track of the conversation when MacKensie turned away from him and the light glinted off the long expanse of bare skin. That damned gown. If he touched the smooth, silky skin on her back one more time, he was liable to yank the straps down and scoop her breasts into his hands. Just the thought made him harden.

"Don't you agree?" MacKensie looked over her shoulder at him and met his gaze. Within the space of one breath, her brown eyes darkened as she caught his heat. She licked her lips, and he remembered how that soft mouth had felt around his cock last night.

"Ahem." His mouth quirking, Uncle Andrew rose to his feet.

Politely, Alex did the same and glanced down to see that MacKensie's face had turned red. He stroked a finger down her cheek, watched it darken further, and tried not to laugh when she glared at him.

"I need to find my Serena before she buys out the auction room," Andrew said. After looking at the crowd of people in the room, he clapped Alex on the shoulder. "You've done a nice job here." Then his gaze dropped to the little vet attempting to straighten Butler's bow tie and laughing when the dog managed to sneak in a lick.

Andrew nodded. "Very, very nice."

✧ ✧ ✧ ✧ ✧

All this socializing could exhaust a girl, but the evening was almost over. And she'd done really well. Smiling a little, Mac leaned forward and checked her makeup in the powder-room mirror. Whatever that beautician had used on her must have been industrial-strength. Even the lipstick had lasted.

She straightened up and turned one way, then the other. The evening gown rippled and glinted. Had Cinderella felt like this? Hopefully glass slippers were more comfortable than these gorgeous, strappy, high-heeled sandals. Her sneaker-wearing feet had gone into shock at least two hours ago.

After smiling at the other women lined up in front of the mirrors, Mac gave herself one last approving nod and headed out.

The tiny hallway that led to the ballroom was empty except for a beefy, middle-aged man. To Mac's surprise, he stepped directly into her path.

"Excuse me." She moved to the side.

He blocked her again. "Now don't you just look a sight? Who would have thought the whore who serviced an Iowa vet convention would be working here? You got some sort of hard-on for vets?" He grabbed her arm, squeezing painfully. "What? Don't you recognize me? You should. I paid you enough, and like I told your pimp, you were a lousy lay."

She froze, cold seeping into her as if the hall had frozen, turning her bones to brittle ice. *Ajax staking out the alley. Man after man from the convention. She'd been so tired. The last man—this man— complaining. Ajax's fists.*

"You've come a long way from that dirty little brat in Des Moines." The fat pockets around his eyes squeezed together as he looked her over, his gaze lingering on her cleavage. "You look good. Very good."

After the first month or so, she'd stopped really seeing the johns. They'd just been shadows that used her body and gave her money so Ajax wouldn't beat her. But she recognized this brutal man. She swallowed, trying to think. What could she say to make him disappear?

"Tell you what." He pulled her toward him. "I'll get us a room upstairs. You can show me if your skills improved along with your appearance."

"No." Her lips felt numb, but her voice didn't waver.

"Oh yes." He yanked her close enough to breathe in her ear. Nausea knotted her stomach. "You're a whore; you can't afford to be picky."

I'm not a whore. Never. Ever. Again. With all her strength, she yanked her arm out of his grasp, ignoring the way his fingernails ripped her skin. "I'm not a whore, you bastard," she hissed. "Stay away from me."

Behind her, the bathroom door opened, and two elderly women exited, one carrying a teacup poodle.

Mac's heart thudded against her ribs like blows from a fist as she turned to them. "Excuse me, but could you show me where the auction room is?"

"Of course, dear," one said.

"Lovely." Mac forced a smile and sidled closer. "That's an adorable dog," she said to the woman holding the poodle. "What's his name?"

"This is Figaro." As she stroked the dog's head, the old woman glanced at the man. "Dr. Dickerson, how pleasant to see you."

"Nice to see you, Mrs. Johnson."

Walking beside the women, Mac passed Dickerson. Even without looking, she could feel the anger radiating from him.

As they left the hall, Mac cleared her dry throat. "Are you acquainted with that veterinarian?" He must be a vet if he'd been at that Iowa convention.

"Oh yes." Mrs. Johnson lowered her voice. "I shouldn't say anything, but"—she glanced at her friend, who nodded—"I hate to see any innocent animal in his hands. He's competent enough, but his temper... He actually struck my poor Figaro once. Just for growling."

He'd struck her too, Mac thought. Before shoving her at Ajax and demanding his money back.

She managed to continue the conversation until well into the busy ballroom. After they pointed to the auction room, Mac veered off, working her way around the side of the ballroom toward where she'd left Alex talking with the mayor. She checked over her shoulder every few seconds, but the man hadn't followed.

Before she'd even managed to get halfway around the room, dizziness surged through her. Head spinning, she staggered to the wall and dropped into a chair. Her face felt cold, then hot, and for a moment her stomach almost revolted. Breathing through her teeth, she fought the sickness down. One breath. Another. She'd used the technique before, especially in the beginning, when she still thought of herself as a nice girl.

She finally mastered herself, although the taste of bile lingered. When a waiter passed by, she waved, and he provided her with a glass of wine from his tray. She downed it quickly, and the sharpness of the chardonnay eradicated the sickness.

Why couldn't there be anything to eradicate her memories as nicely? After using the little napkin to wipe her clammy hands, she rose to her feet. Still no sight of Dickerson, but any glimpse of a big-boned or ruddy-faced man sent fear stabbing through her. Every cell in her body urged her to run and hide.

She hauled in another long breath. *I'm braver than this. I'm not a teenager anymore.* She brought to mind Alex's mother, who wielded intimidation and dignity like weapons of war and moved like the slow freighters that crossed the Sound with unstoppable power. Mac took one step, then another, and caught the regal rhythm. She concentrated so fiercely on being a freighter that she could almost hear the waves lapping against her sides.

The relief when she spotted Alex almost sank her boat.

Tears burned her eyes, and her legs wobbled so much, she had to stop. Thank God, his conversation kept his attention. *Breathe. Breathe.* And then she pushed off again. *I'm a freighter just like Victoria.*

When she reached Alex, he curled an arm around her waist, continuing to talk with a tiny old woman who wanted the feral-cat people to spay the cats running wild around her apartment complex.

When the woman walked away, Alex turned to Mac. His brows drew together, and his eyes narrowed. He tilted her chin up. "What's wrong?"

"Nothing."

The frown deepened and so did his voice. "Do not lie to me, pet."

How could she tell him? Just the thought of that man grabbing her in the hallway… Suddenly she couldn't bear being touched at all. She shoved Alex's hand away and stepped back.

She was surprised that he let her, and even more surprised when he stayed out of her space.

"Breathe, sweetheart," he said softly. His gaze burned across her face before he handed her Butler's leash. "Watch over him for a minute, and then I'll take you home."

He headed for one of the organizers of the event, leaving her with Butler. She stared after Alex until she heard a whine, and a cold nose touched her fingers.

She sank down, her gown ruffling around her feet. "Butler," she whispered. "I'm glad you're here."

His tail wagged, and he pushed his muzzle against her stomach, his warmth more comforting than any heating blanket. Animals never turned on her. Never judged her. Never tried to use her.

Feet stopped beside Butler. Dress shoes, black slacks.

Oh please. No. Mac froze, her fingers tightening on the leash. She looked up into Alex's intense blue gaze, and relief weakened her legs until she clutched at Butler for support.

Alex held out his hand and waited, not trying to grab her, just offering support.

Alex. This is Alex. She took his hand.

Chapter Sixteen

Once they reached home, Alex watched MacKensie remove Butler's costume with fingers that trembled so badly, she could barely unbutton the collar and tie.

When finished, she gave Alex a flickering glance before averting her eyes. "I'm going to bed. All this socializing exhausted me." Her lips tried to curve and failed. "Thank you for taking me." Her progress up the stairs looked like an escape.

Butler obviously thought so also, and he whined long and low.

Alex ran a hand down the dog's head. "Not just yet, guy. Let's give her a little time, and then we'll see what we can do."

After a shower, Alex put on a robe, then waited an hour before he tapped at MacKensie's door. She might want to be alone, but he had no intention of permitting that. Not after seeing the look in her face: fear, not exhaustion.

When she didn't answer, he walked in. The French doors to the balcony stood open, letting in the moist night air scented with the fragrance of sweet autumn clematis climbing the trellis below. A slow rain had begun sometime earlier.

Her back to the room, MacKensie leaned against the railing.

Alex gave the bed a glance. Still made; she hadn't tried to rest. She had looked extremely jumpy earlier, so he spoke from the center of the room to give her warning of his presence. "MacKensie."

She gasped and spun, her instinctive step back stopped by the railing. Damn good thing it was there.

First terror, then recognition. Her muscles eased slightly, and her hands opened, indicating a slight reduction of her nervousness. Not enough. Not nearly enough. His sub was afraid, and that knowledge brought every Dom instinct in his nature to the fore. He walked to the balcony door and stopped. "Come here," he said softly.

Her chin came up slightly, delighting him. "I don't want company now," she said stiffly. "I'm not going to...play."

"I didn't ask you to play. Come here. *Now.*"

Mac felt the cold wrought-iron railing against her hip, preventing any retreat. The soft light from the bedroom lamp outlined Alex's body, leaving his face in shadow and limiting her ability to read his expression or eyes.

She had only his voice. She tightened her fingers around the railing as if that would tighten her resolve, but her defiance withered like an old, unwatered vine, falling dead at her feet. Her knuckles creaked as she opened her fingers and took a step toward him. Another.

He held out his hand but didn't come closer. The way he loomed in the doorway set something trembling in her stomach. He'd push her down, shove his—

"Little sub," he said, his voice deep and gentle, smoothing over the sharp edges of her past. "Are you mixing me up with someone else in your mind?"

So many, many others. Her voice couldn't escape through the constriction in her throat.

His hand closed over hers, warm against her cold. He pulled her closer. "Say my name."

She swallowed. "Alex."

Warm approval washed over her. "Very nice. And what does a sub call her master?"

Master? When had he—

"MacKensie?"

"Sir. I call you 'Sir.'"

"Excellent."

He pulled her into the room, toward the bed, and her feet dragged. An exasperated sound escaped him. "MacKensie, I don't make a habit of bedding women who are terrified. Or freezing. Stand right there."

Without waiting to see if she complied, he fetched her robe from the bathroom and tossed it on the bed. "Hold still." Efficiently, ruthlessly, he stripped off her gown. As he peeled off her panties, she realized they were wet from the rain. Everything was wet, and she shivered as the air hit her bare skin. "Easy, pet," he murmured and, to her relief, bundled her into the long terry-cloth robe, belting it around her with impersonal hands. He hadn't even tried to cop a feel.

"Alex?"

His thumb brushed her cheek. "That's right, little cat. Come with me now." Putting an arm around her, he guided her to the stairs, down and out onto the back patio. Back into the drizzling rain. Next to the Jacuzzi, he stopped. "Don't move," he said again, then uncovered the top. Steam billowed out, the warmth fleeting in the cold night air.

Alex tossed his robe onto a hook on the wall, then added hers, pushing her hands away when she tried to stop him. A chill ran through her. He was naked; she was naked.

"Get in, pet," he ordered, holding out his hand to help her down the steps into the Jacuzzi. Her legs moved like cold blocks of concrete. She gasped when the heat seared her cold skin, and turned to climb back out. He stepped behind her, preventing that move.

"It's too hot."

"You're too cold." He took her hands, then sat down on the seats built into the sides. "Give it a minute."

She stood stiffly in the center of the water, jumping when the jets came on, battering against her. Slowly, slowly, as her body adjusted, her shivers diminished and died.

Alex didn't speak, just held her hands and waited, watching her quietly. The dim glow from inside the house carved hollows under his eyes and cheeks, providing just enough light to catch an occasional blue glint in his eyes.

"Good," he said, just as she realized the water temperature no longer burned. "Sit."

"I'm not a dog." She tried to pull her hands away, as useless an action as a Chihuahua trying to win against a Great Dane. Giving in, she let him pull her down beside him. His hands closed on her waist to move her where the bubbling flow of water would massage her back and the knots in her shoulders.

She waited for him to touch her intimately, to grab her breasts. Minutes passed. And then, with a sigh, she leaned back and let the water soothe her.

Sitting next to her, Alex did the same. He had one long arm laid along the rim behind her head. Soon his fingers started to unravel the French braid in her hair. When her hair billowed loose, he grasped her shoulders, ignoring her start and attempt to withdraw, and turned her so her back was to him.

And then he massaged the rest of the knots out of her shoulders and her neck. When he didn't try anything more intimate, she relaxed again, letting him touch her. Muscles she didn't know were tight complained and then went limp.

"That's better," he said finally and simply set her back in her place so she could lean against the side.

Toenails clicked on the patio, barely audible over the shushing sound of the jets as Butler crossed to the Jacuzzi. He licked her cheek once, accepted a kiss on his nose in return, and then padded back inside the door and out of the rain.

Animals gave simple acceptance and caring, but men always took advantage. Her thoughts stumbled as if hitting a rut in the road. Jim hadn't. And Alex hadn't. She'd been so cold and alone, and he'd taken care of her. MacKensie's eyes burned with tears, and she blinked furiously.

Instinctively she stood. She needed to find somewhere to hide—to cry.

"My sub doesn't cry alone," Alex said softly. "She cries in my arms." He pulled her onto his lap and against his chest.

She couldn't... But his embrace was unyielding, and she couldn't hold it in. A sob welled up from deep inside. It hurt and tore through her throat like the man's appearance had torn through her dreams. Another sob followed and another. *Why, God? I only wanted to have a new life. To be free from the past. But life isn't fair—never, never fair.*

She cried until her throat was raw and her eyes swollen. When she finished, she lay limp against Alex's chest, listening to his slow heartbeat as he stroked her hair. He'd never said a word.

After a minute, he handed her a napkin from the side of the tub. She wiped her tears away and blew her nose.

Grasping her chin, he tilted her face one way, then the other, examining her. "Better. Now tell me what happened at the dance."

She shook her head.

"Something from your past?"

Her mouth tightened over the words that strained to come out.

He sighed, but his eyes never left her face. "MacKensie, unless you tortured small fuzzy animals or children, I can forgive you. Tell me."

The thought of seeing disgust on his face pierced her insides with ice. To have him look at her like the people in Oak Hollow had—like that man just had—she wouldn't survive that. "I will never, ever tell you," she said, her voice hoarse. "Don't ask me again."

He studied her for a long minute. "We'll work on it at a later time."

"No," she whispered. Yet when he pulled her back against his chest, she didn't resist at all.

"Poor little sub," he murmured. "So many worries and so little trust."

Slowly, ever so slowly, the feeling of his arms around her became more than just comfort. Not because of anything he did, but as the upheaval from her past faded, her body remembered the present. And what joy she'd found here in his embrace. Her hands stroked down his back, releasing tiny bubbles against his skin that tickled her palms. She ran her fingers down his spine, fingered the vertebrae between the long muscles, and returned to the hard-packed muscles covering his scapula and upper arms. When she pulled back, she saw a faint smile on his face.

His hand moved to her breast. When her nipple bunched under the touch of his fingertips, his smile increased.

She sighed as the dawning need tightened like a noose around her, squeezing her into urgency. She wanted to have sex with someone who cared and someone she cared for. She needed to make all those memories of other men go away. Her hands slid to his front, and she squeezed his growing cock until it stood erect.

He chuckled and started to lift her up, and she realized he intended to put her hips on the pool rim at a nice level for his mouth.

"No." She shook her head and gasped when his hand slid between her legs, finding her wet already. "I want—I need you inside me. Now." His finger slid over her clit, and she whimpered at the surge in her blood. "Please. Sir?"

He set his other hand against her face. "Do you realize how difficult it is to say no when you call me that and look at me like this?" His hand tangled in her wet hair, holding her for his kiss. His lips expertly teased hers, his tongue as possessive as the finger that slid into her vagina. When her tongue entered his mouth, and he sucked on it lightly, she moaned and pulled back. "Please, Sir?"

She moaned again when he withdrew his finger from her pussy.

"All right, then, little cat." When she made a move to straddle his legs, he chuckled. "I don't think so. Stand up." He pushed her to the side of the Jacuzzi that lacked a seat. Grasping her hands, he placed them on the rim. "Bend over."

Her fingers pressed into the cold, rough concrete. The rain hadn't stopped, and cold drops splattered on her face and back.

Standing behind her, Alex put his arms around her, and his hands closed over her breasts. He played with her, lifting her breasts in his big hands, rubbing her nipples with his thumbs until the peaks turned as hard as the cement under her fingers.

Dammit, she wanted him inside now. She wanted to be engulfed by him, have him drown out her memories so she could pretend no one else had ever touched her. She pushed back and rubbed her bottom against his erection.

He stilled, then bit her neck, his teeth pressing down on the muscle. She remembered when just that had almost sent her over, but not tonight. Tonight too many other things filled her head. That man had touched her. Her mouth had been… She pushed back again, more frantically.

"What you need and what you want aren't the same things," he murmured in her ear, "but you're going to get both tonight." His warm breath made her shiver despite the heat of the water.

He entered her in one merciless thrust, lifting her to her toes. Filling her fully, painfully. She cried out, and her hands clenched on the rim, abrading her fingers. Cold rain sluiced over her shoulders and arms, which were out of the steaming water. He thrust into her once again, and she pushed back. *Take me. Make me forget.*

Suddenly his hands slid lower to touch her intimately, and need sizzled through her, shaking her control, entering her soul. She didn't want to feel anything that deeply, not tonight. She started to straighten.

"Keep your hands on the rim," he growled. She froze.

Still embedded in her, he pushed her legs apart until they gaped widely and she had to hold the rim for balance. His hips pushed her forward, closer to the wall, and then his hand covered her mound—her bare, hairless mound. The sensation was startling. She wiggled up and down on his cock. "Move," she whispered.

He ignored her, anchoring her against him with the hand pressing against her pelvis. The other hand touched something on the Jacuzzi's side. When he moved his hand away from her mound, she realized what he'd done. A jet of water hit her directly on her pussy, and the forceful streams of water felt like tiny fingers flickering all over her clit and labia. She jumped and tried to move back.

"Don't move, little cat," he said, his hips keeping her in place. He secured her further, one hand over her breast, the other right above her mound.

"I don't..." The water demanded a response, and her clit tightened. "I don't want this, Sir."

"I know, sweetheart. That's why I didn't give you a choice." With a finger on each side of her clit, he opened her labia, exposing her completely to the throbbing water.

"Uuuuh," she moaned, unable to move away from the barrage.

And then he started to move inside her, his cock dragging over sensitive tissues, wakening her nerves from inside. Each relentless thrust raised her up on her toes and moved the water up and down her clit like stroking fingers. Inside her, need grew, blossoming along her nerves. Her legs started to shake as her vagina clamped tighter around him. She panted, breathing the cold, moist air that warmed as their movements stirred the water. Tendrils of steam curled around them.

Then his thrusts changed to a forceful rhythm, one that overwhelmed her mind and her emotions, leaving only sensation after sensation. Her clit engorged, growing more and more sensitive, but she couldn't seem to go over. She balanced right on the precipice until every breath came out a whimper.

With a merciless grip, he pushed her closer to the jet, then twisted her hips back and forth in front of the pulsing water. The stream of water hit her clit and then was gone. He turned her back, and water pounded across her for a second. With each twist, he shoved deeper inside her.

Nothing could fight against that. Her clit tightened until it felt as if he'd clamped it between his fingers, and then everything inside her uncoiled violently, shooting pleasure through her in jagged, excruciating waves.

With a low laugh, he slammed into her, keeping her spasms going and going, until his fingers dug into her hips and his thick cock jerked inside her as if her orgasm had compelled his.

Battered inside and out, she leaned on her hands, realizing he must have pulled her back from the jets when she came.

His hands caressed her breasts as he kissed the side of her neck. She'd given him what he wanted, but it seemed as if she'd given him her soul with that orgasm. Now her defenses lay shattered, and she stood there, vulnerable. Exposed. When he pulled out of her, she wanted to cry, but nothing remained inside her.

He didn't try to talk. He simply lifted her up and out of the Jacuzzi and bundled her into her robe. He actually carried her up the stairs to his room, dried her gently, made her drink a glass of water, and pulled her into his arms, never leaving her alone for a second. As she'd wanted, he engulfed her with his presence and the sense of safety he carried with him.

She woke once during the night, curled in a ball with her back against his chest. His hand cupped her breast. Knowing he was asleep, she whispered, "Thank you."

She was shocked when he nuzzled the back of her neck and murmured, "My sub, my pleasure."

She fell back asleep knowing how a kitten must feel in a pile of its brothers and sisters.

Chapter Seventeen

The next day, Mac drove Alex's spare car to downtown Seattle.

Lacking the money to extend her lease, she'd returned her rental car. When Alex caught her poring over maps of bus routes, he'd insisted she use his BMW. Stubborn bastard.

Just like Alex, the car both terrified and thrilled her. She shut the door and patted the BMW's sleek hood. Unlike Alex, the car handled like a dream.

She looked around at the wet streets and tall buildings. The gray day suited her mood perfectly. A thin drizzle of rain plastered her hair to her face and dampened her jeans as she strolled the streets.

Just as the sun came out from behind the clouds, she discovered an odd little park that spanned the freeway. There, she perched on a slab of concrete to eat the lunch she'd bought and watch man-made waterfalls cascade over numerous blocks of cement. The jubilant noise of the water almost drowned out that of the freeway.

As the sun glistened off the wet bushes and warmed her shoulders, she sighed. Time to decide what to do next. So many problems, so little time…

Meeting Dickerson last night had pretty much screwed up her plans for living here. Just thinking about him made her skin crawl. She studied the water, how it splashed down and into the dark pools at the base of the blocks. Perhaps she should give up on living in Seattle. Since she hadn't sold Jim's house, she could go back to Oak Hollow and make some money, then choose a different city for her fresh start. Wrapping her arms around her legs, she rested her chin on her knees. That would solve the problem this time, but there was no guarantee this wouldn't arise again. She had an unsavory past that apparently could surface at any time. Wasn't that lovely?

If she didn't leave…

She breathed past the clenching in her stomach and tried to be logical. *C'mon, Mac. Use your head.* What could the guy do, after all? Announce her previous occupation to the world? Publish her past in the *Seattle Times?* Not likely.

So. He'd shaken her up a bit. She shook her head and attempted a laugh through the tightness in her throat. *A bit?* He'd scared the shit out of her, made her sick, and now Alex probably wondered if she didn't have a screw loose. But hey, she'd turned the bastard down and gotten away. She deserved a major award for not having a hysterical crying fit right there in the ballroom.

But really, Dickerson couldn't do her any harm. And if, God forbid, she ran into him again, she'd be a lot smoother about blowing him off. Her lips curled at the phrase. Not blowing him, but blowing him *off. Heh-heh.*

That's sick, Mac. She shook her head and grinned. *But okay, then. I'm staying here.*

She took a bite of her sandwich. Tuna on sourdough and filled with so many veggies, she had to squish it to get her mouth around it.

Next problem. The BDSM stuff. Her body warmed as she remembered last night and how Alex had controlled her, stripped her, taken her…and held her. His voice, his hands, just his sheer authority, had kept her from any real protest.

Being taken over like that was pretty scary…and pretty cool. Having Alex in control meant she didn't need to be. Didn't need to think, didn't need to worry about what to do or if she performed adequately; he'd make sure she did what he wanted. Something about that kind of mastery seemed to turn her head off and let her body just *feel*—at least so far. So BDSM stuff could go into the "explore further" category.

What about Alex? Just as the thought of the other man had made her sick, the thought of Alex sent warmth through her and gave her a little flutter in her stomach. Setting the sandwich down, she pulled in a breath. Really, Alex was far scarier than the BDSM stuff. Everything he did pulled her closer, bound her to him.

She wasn't exactly fighting getting closer. Beyond just the sex, she liked him as a person, liked his commitment to the little companies he helped start and to the animals he considered in his care. His friends were diverse and honorable and fun, and that said a lot about Alex right there. He had a temper—she remembered his face when Steel had almost hit her—but he controlled it and not the reverse. Majorly bossy...and protective and caring.

She pressed a hand to her stomach. Frak, the man had sucked her right into caring for him.

Before they'd become lovers, she'd known she liked him more than was wise. And the liking had deepened when she gave herself to him.

He could hurt me badly.

She rubbed her hands over her face and sighed. *But what in life doesn't hurt?* Losing Jim and Mary had devastated her, but even if she'd known what would happen, she wouldn't have given up her time with them. Taking care of animals had taught her that. To live without the little fur balls was unthinkable, even when you knew their lives were so much shorter than your own.

And so it would be with Alex. He didn't want a real relationship. He was ritzy and rich and way out of her class. So she already knew the ending to this journey. But being with him was worth it.

She'd walk the path until she reached the end.

❖ ❖ ❖ ❖ ❖

Alex jotted down another note. *If the bookstore added some*—The phone rang. He reached across his desk and picked it up. "Fontaine." *Maybe specializing in*—

"Excuse me." A tenor voice. "I was given this number to contact MacKensie Taylor."

Alex glanced at the caller ID and paused. A Midwest area code. *Oak Hollow Veterinary Clinic.* Well, now… "This is where she's staying," he said. "Did she used to work with you?"

"Well, no. Yes." The man gave an exasperated laugh. "She worked for Jim, the previous owner of the clinic, and came in to help out now and then when I got overloaded. Can I leave a message for her?"

"Of course."

"My name is Brent Goodwin. I have a check for the days she worked last month. I need to know if she wants me to mail it there or hold on to it for her." Brent hesitated. "Do you know if she's planning to return to Oak Hollow?"

How much snooping could be justified under the Dom/sub relationship? *Definitely more.* Alex leaned back in the chair, his eyes on the ceiling. How to finesse some information from an innocent vet? "I got the impression that she felt relieved to be able to leave…after Jim's death," he said delicately. Dammit, was Jim a lover or just a—

Brent sighed. "Yeah, she was pretty happy to get out of here. Poor girl. She spent half a year buried in that house taking care of the old guy as he withered away to nothing. Anyway, I figure she might need this check, so if—"

"She does seem oddly short of cash for a vet," Alex interrupted. "Did she run up a gambling debt or something?" He grinned at the sputter of outrage on the other end of the line. People from small towns weren't nearly suspicious enough.

"MacKensie stepped in to help Jim with his medical bills. And then near the end, he couldn't be left alone, so Mac hired someone to stay with him when she needed to get groceries or pick up prescriptions. We would have helped, but if you know her, you know how much pride she has. And she sure wouldn't take a cent from anyone in Oak Hollow."

Why not, dammit? Alex didn't ask the question. He got the feeling Brent wouldn't share that information. "Well, that's good to know," he said simply. "I'm relieved my high opinion of her is justified."

"Damn straight. She's a fine woman, no matter—" Brent huffed a breath. "I've got to go. Tell her to call me, please." He hung up.

Now that was an interesting conversation. Alex put his feet up on a bare corner of the desk, turning the phone over and over in his hands. Brent considered the little cat generous and loyal. No new information there. And her friend Jim had been old. Alex could feel the tension in his gut ease. She wasn't mourning an old lover, but probably a father substitute.

However, Brent wasn't old, and he wanted her back.

MacKensie didn't want to return. Whatever had happened to her in the past had happened in Oak Hollow. And everyone there knew about it. And had judged her.

Dammit, little cat. How could he help if he didn't know what had happened?

Mac folded her hands in her lap and prepared to be brilliant, charming, and dedicated. Again. If this interview stuff continued much longer, she'd take a nice dive off the horrendously high Aurora Bridge.

Across the desk, Susan Weston grinned. "Don't look like that. We've met before, remember?"

Mac's lips curved. Susan was as high energy, charming, and blunt here at the Weston Animal Hospital as she had been at the ball. "I didn't want to presume upon that introduction," Mac confessed. "Alex is very kind, but—"

Susan snorted. "Alexander Fontaine can be kind, but he's also a hard-nosed businessman and utterly ruthless when it comes to protecting animals. The fact he introduced you as a vet means he checked your background and found you more than competent. Otherwise he'd never have mentioned your occupation."

Mac blinked in surprise. Well, yes, she knew Alex had called her references before letting her stay with Butler, but the fact that he might not have introduced her if he didn't consider her competent, and people knew that... Perhaps she didn't know him that well after all.

"You've never seen him in action, have you?" Susan huffed and amended quickly, "I mean, action related to animals. He's actually put two or three vets out of business."

"Really." Well, God knew she'd seen his temper.

"Oh yeah." Sandy smiled. "And seeing you with Butler didn't do you any harm. That dog doesn't fawn over many people. After meeting you, my partners and I kept an eye on you that night. Animals like you." She spread papers out over the desk. "We, of course, checked your credentials and references. We took a vote this morning, and we'd like you to come to work here."

Mac's breath stopped.

"If things work out, then we'll talk about buying in and all that." Susan rose and held out her hand. "Are you interested?"

Do not scream. Do not do happy dance until get home. "I researched you too, and you're at the top of my list." Mac stood and shook Susan's hand firmly. "I accept."

Chapter Eighteen

"Uh, I don't know... I'm tired and..." Mac's heart rate increased when Alex pushed the dungeon door open and the scent of leather drifted out. The lights in the sconces flickered over the St. Andrew's cross, the benches, the wall of whips and floggers. All that equipment gave an entirely different impression when you had a Dom beside you than when you were just exploring. She shivered as she realized he could and would use all the equipment in here.

Her excuses only caused his grip on her wrist to tighten as he pulled her into the room.

Damn. She should have been warned yesterday when he'd looked up at her and said, "*You realize dragging your Dom off to have sex isn't the usual behavior of a submissive, even when celebrating.*"

It had been a fine, fine celebration. She shivered a little just remembering how she'd straddled him and ridden him like a cowgirl. Yeah, she might have gotten away with jumping him and being so demanding. He'd enjoyed himself as well, after all.

But then when he'd told her they would attend his mother's supper party, she'd refused. Flat-out refused. And oh boy, apparently he'd make her pay for it today.

Did she really want to let him do this domination stuff? At just the thought, her insides started to melt like ice cream in the sun. Frak, she was so screwed.

He put her in the center of the room and gave her a look from determined blue eyes. Dom eyes. "Don't move."

Her breath quickened.

From the cupboard, he removed several things and put them into his pockets. He picked up a set of wrist cuffs, then returned to stand in front of her. "Strip."

All those men she'd undressed for and never felt a thing, but with this man—just that tone of voice made her nipples tighten to aching points. She pulled her T-shirt off, threw her bra on top of it, and wiggled out of her jeans and panties.

When she stood naked before him, he nodded approval, then walked around her slowly. Inspecting her. Rather than try to hide, she raised her chest and her chin. And wished he'd touch her.

"You're a beautiful woman, little sub," he said quietly. His words created a warmth inside her and increased her desire to be touched. He stopped behind her, buckled on the wrist cuffs, and clipped them behind her back before turning her to face him. The feeling of helplessness made her wet, an effect she still couldn't understand, but it didn't seem to matter. Not when he looked at her like this, a faint smile on his lean face.

"Hold still," he warned before he bent and took one nipple in his mouth. Hot and wet.

She jolted backward, earning herself a brisk slap on the side of her thigh. And the sting sent little claws into her clit. Biting her lip, she planted her feet and kept motionless.

His lips demanding, he sucked on her nipple until it peaked, long and taut. From his pocket came a breast clamp: tiny sparkling jewels and bells on a chain below the tweezerlike prongs.

Her mouth dropped open. He hadn't used those since the club.

He fastened the clamp over her nipple, sliding the little ring upward until she tried to retreat from the pain. He left it there for a heartbeat and then loosened it. The pain changed to a pinch that throbbed with every beat of her heart. When he did the other, she realized the biting ache made her aware of her breasts...constantly.

He stepped back, his gaze on her face, and he smiled. "Spread your legs," he said softly.

She bit her lip. She knew he wouldn't really, really hurt her, but with her hands cuffed behind her back, it seemed...

"Now."

Her feet moved apart. He gave a nod and then touched her down there. The sensation of his hand against her bare pussy still startled her. His fingers slid very, very easily across her folds, showing she was very, very wet. His eyes held amusement. "I thought you'd enjoy having clamps again."

"Alex," she whispered, not having any idea of what she wanted to say. His expression didn't change, yet she could feel his disapproval, and she hastily said, "Sir. May—"

He held up his hand, and she bit back her words. He shook his head. "You do not have permission to speak. In fact..." From his pocket, he pulled out a leather gag.

"Wait."

"Open." He put the thick strip of leather into her mouth and tied it behind her head. "If you need to stop, you may either yell or scream. Three times in a row is your safe word, or you can squeeze this." He tucked one of Butler's squeaky toys into her cuffed hands.

She felt so strange. Not able to talk. Hands behind her back. Legs apart. Breasts aching. Helpless and scared and excited.

His hand cupped her cheek, and he moved up against her, his body warm and strong. "Do you trust me, little sub?" he asked softly.

Did she? *Yes.* She nodded, and the tightness compressing her lungs eased when his eyes crinkled. "Good girl."

Her gaze caught on the whips and floggers on the far wall. Oh God, how far did he plan to go?

He turned, following her gaze, and huffed a laugh. "You're not ready for any of those, little cat."

Thank heavens. Would he really want to use something like that on her? The fear inside her at the thought mingled with a funny excitement. She met his gaze and saw how he watched her with a faint smile.

"Yes, MacKensie, you'll get a chance to see how they feel someday. But this is not the day." He unclipped her wrists and pulled her over to a square platform about three feet high. "Crawl on," he said quietly.

Her heart picked up as she did. The top was covered with brown leather, smooth and cool under her hands and knees as she assumed a doggy position.

He bent down to look her in the eyes. "MacKensie, I am going to restrain you now. Do you trust me to keep you safe?" His eyes were steady as his hand stroked her hair.

She wanted to give him what he wanted, wanted to please him. Could she endure this? Be brave for him? She closed her eyes. How far would she go for this man? After a second, she sighed and nodded.

"That's my girl," he murmured. "Stay on your hands and knees."

As he buckled on cuffs just below her knees, his fingers kept brushing against her pussy, and the tiny touches kept her constantly aroused. He attached the cuffs to ropes on the table corners and pulled her legs farther apart. Her one attempt to rise was prevented by a stern hand in the middle of her back. Cool air drifted past her inner thighs, touched her wet labia lightly. God, what was she doing with her butt exposed like this?

But somehow the feeling of the cool air on her pussy changed her focus. She couldn't move, couldn't struggle, couldn't even complain or tell him what to do, and slowly her surroundings faded until all she could think about or feel was that open area between her legs.

He squeezed her bottom, and she gasped as his fingers traced down her inner legs to where she had started to throb. The flat of his hand pressed against her pussy, then touched her hip, leaving wetness behind. His way of keeping his promise to only proceed if she was aroused. As if he did anything these days that didn't arouse her.

And being restrained had excited her—really excited her, she realized, as his fingers slicked up and down her folds, as he spread her moisture over her clit. On hands and knees, her butt in the air, her pussy was open and exposed.

Very exposed. She jerked when he slid a finger into her. *Oh God.*

"Give me your left wrist," he said, one warm hand splayed on her ass cheek.

More? He wanted to do more restraints? Suppressing a whimper, she put her weight on her other arm and held her left arm back to him.

"Good girl." He hooked the wrist cuff to her knee cuff on that side, leaving her balancing awkwardly on her knees and only one arm. After moving in front of her, he knelt to where he could meet her eyes. "Anything too tight? Tingling? Numbness?"

She shook her head, losing herself in the blueness of his gaze.

"All right, then." He gripped her shoulders. "I'm putting you into a position where your head rests just over the edge of the table." He patted a leather pad there that she hadn't noticed. "Lay your cheek or forehead on this. Now relax and let me lower you down."

She couldn't smother the whimper this time, but she let her elbow bend and felt him take her weight. He lowered her shoulders down and pulled her hair away from her face as she laid her cheek on the leather pad. As her body tilted, the weights on the nipple clamps shifted, and the unexpected tugging sent streamers of exquisite pain shooting through her.

A second later, he buckled her wrist to the other knee. When he curled her fingers around the squeaky toy, she tried to remember how to breathe, because, frak, this was just plain scary. With her wrists hooked to her knees, she couldn't raise up if she wanted to. Couldn't move her legs. She tried to lower her butt and managed to move it from side to side. The tiny bit of movement made her feel a little less controlled.

He chuckled and patted her bottom, then buckled a cuff on each thigh just below her hips. When something clanked, she twisted her head around, trying to see. He pulled two chains down from a ceiling rafter and attached one to each cuff. When he took up the slack, her butt lifted higher into the air. Most of her weight remained on her knees, but she couldn't lower her bottom at all. He'd taken away her last bit of real movement.

"Is anything too tight, pet?" he asked, once again kneeling in front of her.

Her breath seemed to be coming too fast as she tried to think past the fear. *Too tight*... Nothing cut off her circulation, but every restraint held her securely. Only her head was free to nod.

He caressed her cheek. "I love seeing you in restraints, tied for my pleasure. Open to anything I want to do." His cheek creased. "You're very wet, little cat," he said softly. He kissed her lips, the softness belying the heat in his eyes. When he pulled back, he ran a finger over her lower lips. "Remember, your safe word is three hoots or pressing the squeaky toy."

She nodded. He wasn't lying; she could feel the wetness of her pussy. Nonetheless, she gripped the toy a little more and heard him chuckle.

"I'm pleased you trust me this far," he said. "Now we'll go a step further." He placed a thick, large, blindfold over her eyes, tying it securely behind her head. The last thing she saw was the faint smile on his lips.

Blackness. She almost hooted right then, but he hadn't moved. His hand stayed on the knot behind her head, his fingers laced firmly through her hair. His other hand rubbed her naked back in long strokes. "I'm here, little cat. I want you to trust me. Relax into the ties and the darkness. All you can do now is hear and feel. And since your body is mine to play with, I will decide what you hear and what you feel." His voice had deepened, taken on that Dom authority.

Inside her, something loosened. She couldn't do anything. Maybe she knew she shouldn't do this, that perhaps it wasn't right, wasn't wise, but there was absolutely nothing she could do. He held all the reins.

"That's the way," he said softly and squeezed her shoulder. She heard him rise, and the subtle warmth of his body and breath disappeared, leaving nothing behind. No sound. No touch. Had he gone?

Her body tensed, and at the same time, her heart rate slowed. Couldn't do anything. No control. The straps and cuffs held her in place, confined her, and yet freed her into a relaxation she hadn't felt before. Almost like when he held her so tightly she couldn't move.

Time passed. A minute? More? Then a touch on her cheek. His warm breath touched her ear as he said, "You're doing well, sweetheart. Very well."

He hadn't left her. His hand caressed her cheek; a finger ran over her lips, making them tingle. Making them long for his mouth.

Silence.

A hand slapped her bottom lightly, and she yelped in shock. Then his fingernails skated across her hips, her buttocks. He massaged her cheeks, trailed down the tender inner flesh of her thighs, coming close...so close. *Oh please. Oh yes.* His fingers went deeper, sliding through her folds, grazing her clit in erratic patterns until she could feel it engorging.

She tried to move her hips, to rub against his finger, and even though the chains held her in place, he must have felt her attempt. He laughed and slapped her bottom again. The sting seared right to her clit.

"This is my body to use," he said and thrust a finger into her so hard and fast, she felt like she should go onto tiptoes. But the only thing that moved was the clench of her vagina in shock.

"Your ass is in the air for my pleasure. You'll come when I want you to and not before."

Heat flared through her as his finger moved inside her. But she needed more than just that.

He pulled his finger out and slapped her again on the other cheek. She moaned and then heard nothing. Felt nothing. Again. Her bottom burned from the swats, yet she could feel how wet she'd grown.

Silence. Then a tug on the breast clamps brought her attention back to them, to the aching, pulsing feeling, and the sensation set up a sizzling pathway from her breasts to her pussy. "Such pretty breasts. Your nipples are bright red and plump, little sub." He gently squeezed her breasts, and his thumb brushed over the clamps every now and then, sending stabs of brutal pleasure across her nerves. As her breasts swelled, the clamps seemed tighter, yet the humming pain made her ache down below. Grow needier.

Then he was gone again. *Silence.* A rustle. *Silence.* Her breasts throbbed and matched the pulsing in her clit. Having her butt in the air seemed to make everything worse, as if it waited there to be filled. Wanted to be filled.

The touch on her pussy came from nowhere, jolting her so the chains rattled. A deep laugh as he slid a finger into her, then withdrew.

Then she felt something pushing at her entrance; a second later, it slid smoothly into her. Fat ball, then thinner. Cool and hard like metal. And heavy—when he let go, she could feel the weight leaning on the entrance to her vagina. With her shoulders against the platform, her butt tilted up, just the weight of the dildo kept it in her.

A hand pulled one buttock away from the other. Something cold and wet drizzled across her anus. She squeaked in shock and tried to jerk away and couldn't move anything, not even when something pushed against her tight hole. *Nooo.*

"Your body is mine, MacKensie," he repeated. He squeezed her butt. "This is a very small plug. Now lean back against it." And he didn't wait for her nod or agreement but pushed the thing right into her. Her nerves quivered around it in shock, the sense of fullness so much worse with the dildo inside her too. She moaned.

And he left her there, her openings filled, and quivers running through her. As the shock died, each tremor sent pulsing currents of excitement through her system until she ached with the need to come.

A warm hand pressed on her bottom. A deep voice. "Come for me, MacKensie."

She heard a loud hum and then something pressed against her clit, the vibrations so fierce that her body exploded with blazing sensation, the spasms hitting the hardness inside her and pushing her beyond. She tried to arch, tried to move, and nothing gave.

The humming stopped as she panted in the aftermath of the brutal orgasm.

"Good girl," he said, caressing her and then moving away. Oh God, what was he doing to her? She listened for him, realized she'd been listening, wanting his deep voice, his touch. Her muscles felt limp, but everything held her in place.

And somehow, just that short climax wasn't enough. Her body wanted more.

A touch on her breasts made her jump. Nothing else happened.

Suddenly he pulled the anal plug partway out, then pushed it in. Again and again. Her hands clenched as those nerves reawakened and started to burn with arousal. He switched to the dildo. He slid it in and out slowly, probing until the end found an incredibly sensitive spot. She gasped as heat flared through her.

He chuckled. "That sounded about right." He continued stroking the dildo across that ball of nerves. over and over. Her vagina clamped down as her need spiraled up like a geyser.

"Come for me," he commanded. A hum. The vibrator pressed against her clit, and every muscle in her body went taut. As the vibrations pounded through her and merged with the exquisite torment from the dildo, her body gathered, drowning out everything. *Tighter and tighter.* Everything inside her flamed out of control and she shattered into pleasure. She could hear her screams, muffled by the gag.

"Very nice." He rubbed her bottom, patted it. Silence.

She felt like hot Jell-O in a glass, knowing if he released her, she'd melt all over the platform. A little tremor rushed through her, making her clench around the dildo and anal plug. The spasm ricocheted back and forth between them.

Her heart rate slowed. Her forehead was slick with sweat.

Hands touched her hips. She moaned in protest and got a slap on her bottom that stung all the way into her vagina. The hard, clenching reaction made her moan again.

"This is my body to play with, little cat." Just his voice sent a quiver through her. Frak, he could read a newspaper to her and she'd get hot.

He moved the dildo again, in and out, pressing against that same oversensitive spot, and suddenly the anal plug moved too. Different nerves sparked to life as the two things inside her rubbed in different, conflicting patterns.

She tightened inside, her vagina clenching around the dildo. Her anal muscles quivered, the nerves confused with the unfamiliar sensations. She started to pant as her arousal grew, more and more, harder. Then the dildo stopped, and only the anal thing moved inside her, keeping her arousal high, right on the pinnacle.

"Come for me, MacKensie." The command again. A hum. Vibrations against her clit, erotically painful against her engorged flesh, and the thing in her anus added different sensations as the vibrator swept her into an orgasm and the violent spasms swept from her anus to her clit, back and forth, shaking her so violently, surely the chains would break.

"Good girl."

She whimpered. Her body didn't feel like her own anymore, but his. Yet he didn't hurt her, just forced pleasure upon pleasure on her. Controlling everything.

How could that seem so exciting? So freeing?

He walked around the bench soundlessly, touching her hands, her feet, running a finger under the straps. Checking her circulation, she realized. A warm hand stroked her neck, squeezed her shoulder. Lips brushed her cheek, a finger under the gag moved it slightly to a new place. "You're doing well, little one," he murmured. The platform squeaked a little as he sat down beside her.

She could feel the warmth of his hip against her shoulder. As he stroked her back in long, slow sweeps, the tension drained out of her. Were they done now? But the things were still in her. What was he planning?

Chapter Nineteen

S mooth, smooth skin with a sheen of sweat. He'd worked her hard, and she still had one more to go. Alex tugged gently on the nipple clamps, watching how the erotic pain made her thighs tremble in response. He rose from the platform.

The muscles tightened in her back as her anticipation grew.

When he walked behind her, the scent of her arousal drew his balls up, and he smiled at the wetness gleaming on her inner thighs. He slid the stainless steel dildo in and out of her—just to keep her awake—before removing it completely.

A pleasingly high whine escaped his little sub.

He ran his hands over her curvy ass, raised to just the right level, and then unfastened his pants. His cock sprang free. After listening to her muffled screams as she came each time, he'd turned so hard, he could probably pound nails.

Fisting his cock, he swirled the head against MacKensie's slick folds. He thrust into her, and her hot, wet pussy felt so incredible, he almost came right then. The thin dildo he'd used hadn't prepared her for his thickness, and her shoulder muscles went rigid as he drove deeper into her. He could feel the butt plug and how it increased her tightness.

She trembled under him. Head down, ass up, tied in place—very few positions left a sub so vulnerable. He roughened his voice. "You're tight and hot and wet, little cat, and I've been waiting a long time to take you like this. I'm going to take you hard now...and there's nothing you can do." The clench of her vagina around him told him his words increased her arousal rather than her fear. Excellent.

He squeezed her ass cheeks, letting her feel his strength and her helplessness. Her muscles quivered under his hands, and when he slid his fingers over her clit, she moaned. Needy and wet.

And now, as a Dom, he would take her for his own pleasure.

He started slow, letting her pussy stretch to fit him, and then he took her just as hard as he'd said, drawing out the pleasure for them both.

Something about this position brought out the beast, and he growled as his balls contracted and the need to release increased. He picked up the Hitachi and flipped it on. The loud hum almost drowned out her moan, which sounded equally of excitement and desperation. The vibrator was so strong, he could feel it inside her pussy as he pressed it, gently this time, to her clit. Gripping her hip with one hand, he drove in deeper, his balls slapping against her pussy. He thrust, then pressed the vibrator against her briefly, thrust, pressed—again, and she came so powerfully, the spasms almost pushed him out of her. With a laugh, he tossed the wand aside.

Her pussy clenched around his cock as he secured her hips and plunged into her, letting himself go. His balls tightened, squeezing painfully as if someone had grabbed them, and then his cock erupted in forceful jerks that sent pleasure searing through every nerve in his body.

He stayed in her as his heart rate decreased, enjoying the intermittent contractions that rippled through her vagina. Eventually he took a slow breath and straightened up. He forced his fingers open and winced; she'd have bruises on her hips tomorrow.

Removing the anal plug caused a moan. Withdrawing his cock made her whimper. One by one, he removed the straps and chains, then the blindfold and gag. She blinked at him, her big brown eyes dazed.

"My little sub," he murmured as he picked her up. In the corner chair, he settled down, pulling the blanket from the end table over her. Both of them reeked of sweat, sex, and satisfaction. Her muscles were limp, although an aftershudder would jerk through her now and then. But she snuggled into his embrace in a way that told him his hopes had been justified. Her trust in him had grown.

Had it grown enough?

"Did you like being restrained?"

Mac rubbed her cheek against Alex's chest. Her muscles, her whole body, felt wilted like aged lettuce. If the house started on fire, she'd probably burn before she made it out of the chair.

"MacKensie, answer me."

Restrained. Right. Her wrists and legs hadn't forgotten the feel of the straps, of the bindings holding her in place and how he touched her whenever and wherever he'd wanted. She'd let him do that to her. "I... It was different."

"That isn't an answer." His hand gripped her hair, tilting her head back so she had to meet his intense gaze. "Try again," he suggested. Ordered.

She wet her lips, her mouth dry.

He glanced away, moved his arm from around her to reach the end table, and grabbed a bottled water. She fumbled her arms free of the blanket to remove the top and then drank half the bottle. "I didn't realize I was so thirsty. We hadn't been...uh...messing around that long."

"All that panting." His cheek creased as he smiled, his eyes still slightly heavy from satisfaction, and she felt an answering satisfaction, both from her own orgasms and that she'd obviously pleased him.

When he didn't speak further and just waited, she realized he still expected an answer to his question. Damn the man. "I...I feel funny about it," she finally said. Honesty sucked. She turned her face into his chest and added, "It makes me hot."

"And that bothers you?"

She nodded. He stroked her hair. How could he smack her bottom, pound into her, and then be so comforting right afterward?

"Because you're an independent woman who shouldn't enjoy giving over control to a man. Ever."

"That's it."

"Our society says being dominated is a bad thing even if you enjoy it. But it's not a solely female need, sweetheart. There are a lot of men who enjoy handing over control in exactly the same way."

True. She'd seen men in the submissive positions in the BDSM clubs, with both men and women as Doms. She peeked up at Alex. "You?"

He chuckled and ran a finger down her cheek. "What do you think?"

She considered the power he virtually radiated, the authority in his eyes and voice, and the way he took charge without even thinking. "Never. You'd never give up control."

"Very good." His thumb ran over her lips and rubbed a sore spot the gag had left. "Although I can play nicely with other people most of the time, I am very much a sexual dominant." His lips curved. "And you are a sexual submissive, little cat. Do you realize that?"

Sexual submissive. He'd put a boundary on it. The right boundary. She didn't and wouldn't want to cave in to him or anyone else during the day. Definitely not at work. But other times... When his voice deepened and he said, *Strip*, everything in her wanted to do exactly that—and anything else he ordered. She had wanted him to take her hard, to tie her down, to tease her, and make her beg. Not having to think left her with only the feel of his hands on her, his voice, and the sensations he gave her.

A sexual submissive. "Yes. I see that." The acknowledgment gave her the same paranoid feeling as if she'd left her car unlocked in Pioneer Square. Like she was defenseless, and now he could take what he wanted.

His arms tightened around her. "It works two ways. A submissive gives up her power, yes, and some people consider that a submissive's gift."

"You don't?"

"Not particularly. No more than any trade." He kissed the top of her head. "You have a need to submit, to surrender control, and to give of yourself and body, and being controlled fulfills something inside you." He paused. "I need to dominate, but part of domination is the need to cherish and protect. Everyone in the world has these desires to some extent; we're further to one end of the scale."

That felt right. What she'd done and he'd done. It sure beat thinking that suddenly she'd turned wussy.

"Okay." She could feel her muscles that had knotted with his first question ease. There was more give-and-take in this than she'd acknowledged. And more equality in its own way.

BDSM. All right. She was submissive—and maybe even that way without Alex. But the thought of being without Alex sent a chill through her. She needed to face that too, as long as she was dealing with tough issues. How long was this little interlude going to last?

She licked her lips and forced the words out. "I have a job now."

"Yes."

"Cynthia's in Europe."

"Yes."

And wasn't he just being a world of help in this conversation? "Then aren't the reasons for my being here—living here—gone?"

"Ah." Firm fingers pushed her hair away from her face, raised her chin. "Do you want to leave?"

Just looking at his hard cheekbones, the sun lines beside his eyes, his lips, which held no smile, made her heart quiver, made her want to plaster herself against him. Instead she gave him a nasty look. "My question came first."

He laughed, and then his gaze turned serious. "Stay, little vet."

The words made her heart turn over.

He finished. "Let's see where this goes."

It wouldn't go too far; she knew that. He was rich; she was poor. High society: ex-whore. Stable: neurotic. But for now, there was no place in the entire world that she'd rather be than here in his arms.

Late the next afternoon, Mac edged in the door, juggling her bundles, only to have everything drop except the one thing that might have survived a spill. "Frak, frak, frak." A bark came from the back of the house and then scrabbling sounds as Butler charged toward the foyer to greet her.

To top off the wreck of her day, she heard footsteps. Alex was home.

And this wasn't her home. *What was I thinking?*

Her stomach sank. He'd probably order her right out of his house. The clawing worry in her stomach duplicated the tiny claws digging into her forearm. The kitten had seen Butler.

"Easy, kitling," she murmured. "I don't think he eats cats." But she didn't know, now did she? "Butler," she said firmly. "Behave." She turned so the cat was out of the dog's sight and vice versa.

Alex walked around the corner with that easy grace and power, and her heart did that funny dip like it did every time she saw
him. Maybe she had a heart condition.

"How did the day go?" he asked; then his eyes narrowed, and
he moved forward. "What's wrong, little vet?"

Caught. Caught dead to rights. When she was a kid, she'd rescued
a half-starved puppy and brought it to the foster home. Arlene
had thrown it out. *"This is my home, not yours."* That night, Mac had
sneaked out and found the puppy still in the front yard. So little.
All bones and big eyes. She'd carried him across town to the
animal rescue and cried all the way back. You would think she'd
have learned.

Of course, Alex liked animals. Maybe... Her stomach tightened, and she looked down. Anything to avoid his eyes. This was
Alex's home. Not hers. If he liked cats, he'd have one.

He huffed a laugh, and she looked up in time to get a firm kiss
on her lips. "I'm not sure which of you is shaking harder," he
murmured, disengaging the kitten's claws with an easy competence. "Butler, lie down," he ordered absently when the dog's
approach triggered a tiny hiss.

"I'm sorry," Mac whispered, looking at the antique furnish-
ings. "It's just for tonight, and then I'll try to find him a home. He
was in the middle of Mercer Street, and I couldn't leave him. If
you don't want him in the house, then..." Maybe she could sneak
him into a motel.

He gave her a puzzled look. "MacKensie, if you could have
left a kitten in the middle of the road, then you aren't the woman I
thought you were." He followed her gaze to the antique table.
"But if you're going to bring beasties home—and being a vet, you
probably can't resist—then we'd better move some of this stuff to
the attic."

The sinking in her chest continued through her whole body
until she felt as if she stood in quicksand. "You mean"—she

swallowed and stared at the white kitten purring against his chest—"it can stay? Tonight, at least?"

"Of course." His eyes held both amusement and warmth. "However, if you bring home so many that the house smells like a kennel"—he stepped closer—"I'll have an excellent reason to spank your pretty ass until it's bright pink."

The wave of heat that seared through her took her by surprise.

His lips curved, and he ran a finger down her cheek. "Maybe I won't wait for an excuse," he murmured. But then, as if he had an internal switch to turn off his desire, he stepped back and handed her the kitten. "I assume there's kitten chow in your car?"

She nodded mutely and blew out an exasperated breath as he and Butler headed out the door. *How come he has a switch and I don't?*

❖ ❖ ❖ ❖ ❖

Later that evening, Alex leaned on the door frame and grinned. His little sub sat cross-legged on the rug by the fire, introducing the snow-white kitten to the pleasures of string chasing. Three feet away, Butler lay quivering with eagerness to help. The dog and cat had come to a wary understanding after a few altercations. If Butler sniffed too enthusiastically, he'd get scratched. If the kitten pounced on Butler's tail, it now knew an entire dog would try to play. Alex hadn't laughed so hard in a long time.

From the way she'd been holding her ribs, MacKensie hadn't either. She had a lovely laugh when she really let go, uninhibited and joyful, and it pleased him immensely that over the past weeks, her laugh came more easily and had even descended into adorable giggling once or twice.

With a clever move, the kitten captured the string. Thin tail held high with pride, he dragged his prize off behind a chair.

"Supper is ready," Alex announced.

Mac turned. "You cooked?"

"That's a very parochial attitude," he informed her. "In this enlightened age, men can and do cook."

"Uh-huh." She pushed to her feet. "You might be enlightened—and I'm not too sure about that—but cook?"

"If you must be so literal about it all, Margaret cooked. I heated."

His insubordinate little sub laughed at him, so he pulled her closer and took her mouth. It softened under his, and a quiver slid through her body. He hadn't forgotten the look in her eyes when he had mentioned spanking her. Perhaps he'd bed the animals down somewhere and then bed MacKensie.

He put a kiss on her forehead and let her go. As they headed to the kitchen, the kitten darted ahead, bursting out of hiding to pounce on shoelaces before scampering away again.

Alex tucked an arm around MacKensie's waist, pulling her closer. "*Stay, little vet,*" he'd said on Wednesday without even thinking. But now that he'd had time to think, he felt the same. Women had come and gone in his life—many women—but apparently he'd been waiting for this wary little sub.

As he started dishing up the food, something stung his calf. He looked down to see the kitten climbing his jeans to get to the food.

MacKensie sputtered out a laugh and disentangled the little guy. Holding him even with her gaze, she frowned into the innocent blue eyes. "You've already eaten. Twice." Her gaze shifted to Alex, laughter bright in her eyes. "He's obsessed with food."

Alex held up a tiny piece of crab to the kitten. The food disappeared. The kitten licked Alex's finger clean, then, unsatisfied, sank tiny teeth into his thumb.

Alex yanked his hand away, ignoring the snickering coming from his little sub. He glanced at his thumb. No blood. "Ungrateful feline. You can get your own food next time." He rubbed the upright ears with a finger and sighed as claws latched onto his sleeve and a pink nose checked his hand for more food. "Definitely obsessed with food." Alex glanced at MacKensie. "Since we already have a Butler, I suppose this one can be our Chef and hang out in the kitchen all day long."

She grinned at him. "A chef. Anything to avoid cooking, huh, Sir?"

"You'll suffer for that impertinence, sub," he growled at her.

No fear appeared in her eyes, just a flash of heat. "Oh dear."

As he grinned, satisfaction washed through him. Her trust in him continued to grow. She didn't jump when he touched her unexpectedly; her laughter came more easily. Yet he'd seen the wariness in her eyes when she'd brought the kitten home. She didn't fear him physically any longer, but emotionally?

He'd asked her about her past twice in the last week. The last time, he could see from the growing tenseness in her body, the way she ran her hands up and down her thighs, that she'd wanted to share with him. But her uncertainty had won again.

A little more time he'd give her, and then, if needed, he'd drag her back to the dungeon for another session in trust.

Chapter Twenty

A s the door to the mansion opened, Mac rubbed her clammy hands on her cape and frowned. She'd heard of butterflies in the stomach, but hers felt more like giant birds. With claws. She pressed her hand to her abdomen. *I'm a friendly, competent, pretty woman. I can do this.* She could act like a lady and not humiliate herself or embarrass Alex by doing something gauche. *Piece of cake.*

When she glanced back at their car—again—Alex's arm slid around her waist, preventing any escape. She glared into his amused eyes and managed to put a smile on her face.

"Good evening. Please come in." The butler—a real one— took their coats. He glanced at Mac's attire and didn't—quite— sniff in disapproval.

Mac raised her chin. Alex had wanted to buy her a dress, but she'd refused. She had an adequate dress, after all. A basic black that she'd worn everywhere, ever since her sorority sister Tiffany had tossed it across the room to Mac, declaring she'd never wear the dismal color again.

In the center of the foyer, Victoria turned from the last guest. When she saw Mac, her smile disappeared. And probably not because of the dress.

Why did Alex have to have a mother? *A rich, dignified mother.*

"I'm pleased you both could come," Victoria said, giving her son a kiss on the cheek. "Alex, you know the way."

Mac stopped just inside the room and stared. A huge chandelier cast glimmering light over people dressed in suits and cocktail dresses. The babble of conversation swamped the soft music. Perfume and aftershave scented the air.

"You look lovely, little vet." Alex kissed her fingertips, then nipped one sharply enough to make her squeak. "And when this is over, I intend to strip you out of that pretty rag, bend you over a bench, and take you hard."

Before she'd recovered from the surge of heat at his totally unexpected words, he was introducing her to an older couple. "John, Felicia, this is MacKensie Taylor. She's a vet and working with Susan Weston. MacKensie, this is John and Felicia Lordan. They have three cats from the shelter—or is it four now?"

Just that easily, the conversation took off as Felicia talked about their newest adoptee. Mac gave Alex an admiring glance before attending to the talk.

After meeting more people, Mac turned to Alex. "Most of the people here are high society and politicians, except for the slew of veterinarians infesting the place. Isn't that combination a little strange?"

He grinned. "My mother uses her parties for recruitment. She—" He broke off, his attention on the door.

Pleasure washed through Mac when Peter and Hope entered the room. *Look, I actually know someone in Seattle.*

While the men shook hands, Hope gave Mac a hug, saying, "I hoped you'd come." The small group wandered over to the drink table, presided over by a man in a black coat.

Mac smiled at the bartender before confiding to Hope, "This is the first time I ever met a real butler, but I like our Butler better. Not nearly as stuffy."

"I have noticed that myself."

Mac turned and froze. Alex's mother. *Oh frak. Open mouth, insert foot.*

Alex didn't seem to notice the chill as he laughed and said, "Our staff is growing, Mother. We now have a Chef who spends most of his time in the kitchen." Alex grasped Mac's wrist and turned her arm over to display the scratch marks.

"*Our* staff?" Victoria's eyebrows rose and then snapped together as her gaze turned to Mac. "*You* like *cats?*"

Alex's voice turned cold as he said, "Enough to risk life and limb rescuing a scrawny ball of fluff from the center of Mercer Street."

Mac winced. She'd thought the story of her dramatic rescue of the cat amusing. Instead she had gotten swatted on the butt— really hard—for almost getting killed.

"Well." The chill in Victoria's eyes eased. "Good for you. Far too many people don't like cats."

"I—Well, hell," Alex said and earned himself a real frown from his mother. He held up his hand. "I'm sorry, Mother. I didn't realize I hadn't mentioned it at the ball. MacKensie's a vet. Susan already snatched her up to work at the hospital."

Whoa. The chill disappeared completely, Mac noticed, as Victoria murmured, "A vet. Indeed."

"Here she goes," Alex muttered, and then the full force of the woman's personality came to bear on Mac.

"Alex is obviously quite amiss in his introductions. I presume he neglected to tell you that I run a cat rescue."

Mac's jaw dropped. "You?"

"Me. One of the finest in the state. And we have many, many veterinarians"—she glanced around the room with a smile—"who volunteer to help spay and treat our residents." Victoria tilted her head and waited.

Frak, the woman was way too much like her son. "I... Well, I just started working, but...I'd be delighted to volunteer as soon as I know my schedule." Actually she would. She'd put in many hours back home doing just that. Her smile felt natural this time. "I really would be happy to help."

"Excellent. You'll have to invite me over to meet...Chef." Victoria accepted a drink from the bartender with a nod of thanks. "Such names." She shook her head. "A few years back, I instructed my son to get a butler for his parties." She took a sip of her drink, nodded approval at the bartender. "Perhaps I might have indulged in a slight amount of nagging."

Mac kept her mouth from dropping open. The regal posture couldn't hide the laughter dancing in Victoria's blue eyes.

"As you might have discovered, MacKensie, Alex doesn't respond well to orders."

"Um. No. He reacts rather badly." Mac felt a flush creeping up her face. Just this afternoon she'd instructed him to relax rather than building a cat condo. He'd gagged her and cuffed her to a patio post. What kind of man had anchors embedded in posts?

"Exactly," Victoria said. "So I was quite pleased when he said he'd found a fine butler."

Mac choked back a laugh as she realized what his mother meant.

"You laugh?" Victoria raised her eyebrows. "I'll have you know, when we were introduced, that incredibly ugly Butler of his *licked* my *ankle*."

Oh Lord, she could just see it. Mac couldn't keep the giggles down.

With a tilt of her head and a smile, Victoria excused herself to see to her guests.

Hope grinned. "Just when I think she's made of ice, she proves me wrong."

Mac felt a tiny upwelling of hope. Maybe Alex's mother didn't hate her after all. As the others ordered drinks from the bartender, Mac watched Victoria make the rounds, and she realized the woman intimidated every damn person she talked to. Even the congressman.

For the next hour, with either Hope or Alex at her side and eventually by herself, Mac mingled and nibbled on hors d'oeuvres, argued about Seattle and Washington politics, and gossiped about celebrities. She was actually having a good time, she realized. Although a bit conservative, the guests were, without exception, intelligent and involved.

Could life get any better? She had a whole new world here, with a job and a lover and friends. Time to call the real estate agent back in Iowa and get her house listed for sale.

Smiling a little, she turned and came face-to-face with Dickerson. She gasped.

His wet lips drew up in a satisfied smirk. Grabbing her wrist, he leaned toward her. "Want to change your mind, slut?"

The blood drained out of her head, leaving her dizzy. This couldn't be happening.

"My bitch of a wife might have left me"—the enraged, sick look in his eyes made Mac's stomach twist—"but I'll have you to service me every night."

Her mouth filled with bile, but her answer was engraved in her very bones now. "No, I won't."

"You're nothing." Dickerson pulled her closer.

What would it take to make him leave her alone? Insults? "I may be nothing, but you're really little. And the worst I ever had." Her voice wasn't loud, but people's heads turned at the emotion in it. More turned when she wrenched her arm out of his grasp. "Stay away from me."

His face turned a horrible purple. "Cunt. You don't belong here among decent people," he said, then raised his voice. "Victoria, this woman is a whore. She's from the Midwest, where she worked out of an alley, servicing anyone who'd give her money."

Shocked inhalations filled the air, each sound stabbing through her defenses, until she wondered why there wasn't a pool of blood at her feet. She staggered back a step and tore her gaze from his, only to meet the barrage of eyes. Condemning, disgusted.

Victoria, her mouth pinched thin. Hope, with her hands over her mouth.

Across the room, *Alex*. Eyes like ice, yet filled with fury. He shoved a person out of his way and headed straight for her.

She ran.

The lights of the city never went dark.

Mac stood on the balcony of the third-rate hotel and watched the cars crossing the Ballard Bridge like a jeweled ribbon of light. The saucerlike Space Needle glowed high above the city. How many children thought it was an alien spacecraft coming to steal them away?

"Take me too," she whispered, her hands clutching the railing. She stared up into the night sky, clear of clouds, the stars muted by the city. Surely rain should be pouring from the sky and the air should be cold, to match the aching chill inside her.

How can the world go on when mine has been destroyed?

So many people had attended Victoria's party—all the leaders of this city. The gossip would spread, and then everyone would know about her and what she'd done.

In Oak Hollow, Jim had given her a job because he loved her. But here? Even if she and Susan were friendly, the other vets wouldn't permit an ex-whore to work there. *My job—gone.*

No one else would hire her. *My future—gone.*

Hope's face, the shock on it. *My new friends—gone.*

And Alex. She let go of the railing and wrapped her arms around her stomach, trying to contain the pain. She hadn't even dared to return to the house, even to get Chef.

Alex would have followed her there. Of course he would. And she couldn't bear to see the condemnation in his eyes.

Even if he didn't hate her, their time together was finished. No one associated with a whore.

Her knees gave out, and she slid down to sit, facing the desolate hotel room. A few more tears escaped, but she'd pretty much exhausted that avenue of comfort.

Hadn't been much comfort anyway.

Time to pick up and move on, MacKensie. But her past would bite her in the butt no matter where she went. How could she live like that, knowing someone could take everything from her again?

Maybe she should change her name and face. She gave a short laugh. Plastic surgery cost money, and gee, she didn't have a job. Not anymore. Well, she could possibly try a do-it-yourself facial reconstruction: bash her face into the wall, bust her nose, and let it set crooked. Then cut her hair short, spike it, and dye it black.

What the hell. Why not?

She was a survivor. The past years had taught her that. Knock her down and—eventually—she'd pick herself up and march on.

But this time she'd march without her heart. *Oh God, Alex...* She wouldn't go back for her clothing. No. Just disappear from his life. She rocked back and forth. What would he be thinking now? Would he feel betrayed? She tried to tell herself that he wouldn't care, and kept seeing his face when he held her in the dungeon. *"Stay, little vet."*

How long would he wait for her to return? *Oh please, don't let him be hurt.* Her breath hitched as her throat tightened. Guess she hadn't cried herself out after all.

She heard a key in the lock and looked up.

The hotel-room door opened. A young man in the hotel's uniform glanced at her before turning to someone in the hallway. "You were right, sir. She does look ill. Do you need me to call an ambulance?"

"I'll let you know." Alex stepped into the room. He handed the bellboy several bills. "Thank you for your help." As the man disappeared, Alex closed the door.

Alex, Alex, Alex. His name reverberated in her head with the beat of her pulse. "H-how"—her voice cracked—"how did you find me?" She couldn't voice the real question: *why are you here?*

"Your taxi. We helped start the company. As a courtesy, they keep a car or two on the street for Mother's parties." He bent and hauled her to her feet.

Couldn't she get anything right? Not even an escape? "Alex," she whispered. "No."

His jaw tightened. He pulled her into the room and sat on the bed beside her. His grip moved from her arms to her wrists, a ruthless grip that didn't release when she tugged. "Explain," he said.

She stared down at his corded, muscular hands, at the thickness of his wrists. "You heard him. It's true. I'm a whore."

"And you've been trolling Pioneer Square in your spare time?" He snorted. "I said *explain. This* was what happened twelve years ago. How did you get started?"

She yanked at her hands again without success. Her worst nightmare never included sitting next to Alex and delving into the dregs of her life. "I am not going to talk about it."

"Yes," he said quietly, his voice deepening. Dom voice. "You are."

And he would keep her here until she did. Talking wouldn't be easier an hour from now. Her stomach twisted into a massive, painful knot, and she swallowed hard. The hands encircling her wrists felt more restraining than any leather cuffs. *No escape.* "I ran away. My foster home… When Arlene's daughter graduated, she closed down. The one I went to—the man tried to touch me." Her bitter laugh sounded more like a sob. "I ran from him and ended up under others. Smart, huh?"

His thumbs rubbed the back of her hands, and the tiny comforting gesture made tears pool in her eyes. He couldn't hate her and do that.

"How old were you?"

"Fifteen. Old enough to know better."

"You could have gone back…"

"I'd decided to. But…I was stupid, so *stupid*. I hadn't eaten in three days, and a guy bought me a burger. He said he had an extra room." Alex's hands slid down to hold hers, enfolding them in warmth. "I walked into his apartment thinking everything was going to be all right." *The relief singing through her. Food. A place to stay. A friend. Then the slap, coming out of nowhere.* "He was a pimp. He beat me." *A fist in the stomach. The shocking, horrible pain…*

She tried to smile as she said lightly, "I tried to escape once or twice, but he didn't like that." *The beatings, over and over. Face pressed into the carpet, bleeding, crying.*

Alex's hands tightened around hers, and she heard a low noise, almost like a growl, but when he spoke, his voice was even. Unemotional. "How did you escape?"

"Jim." The memory caught her and pulled her upward. *The sweetness of being cared for, of being loved. Why did they have to die?* "Jim and Mary found me after a…client had expressed his displeasure, and Ajax had…" She licked her dry lips. "They took me in." *Clean. Bandaged. Fed.* But she didn't trust them. She'd already unlocked the bedroom window. "Jim came in and put a puppy into my lap." *Wiggles and joy, soft and trusting.* "I…I was caught."

"How old were you then?"

"Just under sixteen. I had walked the streets about a year."

"They kept you. Helped you get into college. And then you went back to Oak Hollow for Jim."

Her gaze jumped up. "How'd you know that?"

His eyes crinkled, and then his gaze turned cold. "The point is that you should have been the one to tell me."

She should have. Guilt seared through her so fast that her eyes teared. She looked down, away, anywhere but at his face. "I'm s-sorry. I should have told you about being a whore. That you'd be going to bed with a—"

"Dammit!" Hard hands gripped her shoulders, and Alex shook her once. "You're not a whore. And you should have told me because you share painful things with your Dom—and your lover. I thought you'd been raped, for God's sake."

"Not rape. I gave it away for money," she whispered, the shame like scalding water.

"Oh, sweetheart." A hand against her cheek turned her face to his. "You were a teenager, which is another term for idiotic. You jumped from bad into worse, but that wasn't your fault. Hell, even if you took money for sex and had a good time doing it, that's not something I'd hold against you." A crease appeared in his cheek. "I know too many women—and men—who've married for money, which is essentially the same thing, only with better living conditions." He set her on his lap and wrapped her in his arms.

The sweetness of his embrace made more tears come. But she knew he didn't really mean it. A whore was a whore.

Chapter Twenty-one

His little sub let him hold her, yet he could feel the stiffness of her body against his. She had heard his words, but her subconscious didn't accept them. Her self-loathing was so great that she didn't believe he could care.

But he knew the biggest missing pieces of her past now, and her behavior finally made sense. She'd been as abused as any little puppy or kitten he'd rescued. He could work with her on putting this into balance, but only if she stayed with him. "You know, when you ran from me," he said gently, "when I arrived at home and you weren't there, it felt like you'd ripped my heart out."

Her breathing paused.

"I love you, MacKensie. I would have told you before, but I knew it would scare you." He stroked her silky hair. Such a stiff little body. "Normally at this point, a person might show how much they care by indulging in sex."

He set her on her feet and caught the confused but accepting look in her eyes. She didn't believe he loved her, and although she would let him take her to bed because she needed him as badly as he needed her, she would spend the entire time grieving, convinced he'd leave. He unbuckled her glittery belt and tossed it aside. After unzipping her black dress, he pulled it down to pool around her ankles.

Then he yanked her, facedown, over his lap.

Mac hadn't even managed to regain her breath when his hand landed on her bare bottom. She yelped in shock, tried to get away, but her feet tangled in her dress, and Alex's merciless hand pushed her shoulders down.

Slam. "I love you, MacKensie, and I'm doing this because I love you."

Slam. "I wouldn't do this if I didn't care, but you mean everything to me, and if this is what you need, then this is what you'll get." He added in a mutter, "But we're damned well going to work on changing this association between caring and spanking."

Slam. "I am very angry that you didn't trust me enough to tell me about your past."

Slam. "I am very angry that you didn't trust me to still love you anyway."

Slam. "I love you, little sub, and I'm doing this because I love you." A pause. "MacKensie. Do I love you?"

Her head spun. He couldn't possibly love her. Not with her past. "I'm a whore."

A growl. *Slam, slam, slam.* The pain burned through her, and tears streamed down her face. He rubbed his hand over her burning buttocks. "You were an abused little girl. If Hope said she'd been forced to be a prostitute at fifteen, would you hate her?"

"Of course not!"

"Then don't hate yourself." He slapped her again. "I love you, idiot sub. Do you believe me?"

He'd turned his back on Cynthia. He could easily have done that to Mac, but he was here. He'd followed her and had no reason to do that unless he loved her. He'd let her bring a kitten home, bought her pizza, introduced her to his friends. And his mother. He'd come after her. He could have any woman in the world...but he was here. "I believe you," she whispered.

"Good." His hand came down, cracking across her skin three more times.

Her fingers clawed into the ugly carpet as she cried out, sobbing. "Why?"

"To make sure you didn't forget." His hand didn't release her shoulders, and she tensed, waiting for the next blow. Instead his hand stroked over her back, across her stinging bottom, and into the crease between her buttocks and thighs. Light, feathery touches like a counterpoint to the burning of her skin.

"What are you doing?" She pushed up and had her shoulders shoved right back down. A light slap hit her upper thigh, making her hiss.

"Silence." He bent and yanked her dress completely off her feet, then shoved her feet apart. Cool air struck her pussy, making her shiver. Feeling vulnerable, she tried to close her legs.

He slapped her thigh again. "Do not move, sub."

God, that voice. Something inside her tightened, and she froze. He wouldn't...

A finger stroked down through her folds, finding her only slightly damp. "Did you know that some submissives find a good spanking to be exciting?"

"No way."

That earned her a mild slap on her upper thigh. "I think it's time to work on making your spankings into something more fun for both of us."

Her pussy was open, and now his fingers flickered over her labia, her clit, before returning to rub her tender bottom. The world shifted as arousal sparked to life inside her.

He pushed a finger into her, holding her shoulders down when she jerked. In and out; then, with a slick finger, he rubbed over her again. With each stroke, she could feel the nubbin engorge with blood. Her hips squirmed as he plunged his finger back in, pressing deep, then returned to her clit.

"You see," he murmured, "when you're excited, your body has trouble telling the difference between pain and pleasure." He slapped her butt lightly, and the pain stung, yet sizzled right to her groin. As his thumb slipped into her, he traced his fingers over her clit, then captured it between his knuckles, pressing, releasing, in a rhythm she couldn't escape.

Her vagina tightened around him, needing more. She was getting so close, and then he pulled out. She whimpered at the loss, at the frustration.

Slam. Slam. Slam.

Frak! Shocking, stinging pain, and yet it sent her right to the brink of release. *So close.* She panted, digging her fingers into the carpet.

Yet he didn't touch her. She moaned.

Then he pressed into her again, stroking that spot inside. "Come for me, MacKensie." His fingers rubbed her clit firmly, and with his other hand, he slapped her bottom.

"Oooh, oo, oo, oo." She bucked on him as he plunged his thumb in and out, as his fingers tapped her clit just enough that her orgasm wouldn't stop. His hard hand pressed her down again, pinning her to his knees as he drew every last spasm out of her.

When he finally picked her up off his knees and held her, rocked her, told her he loved her, that she was his wonderful sub, she cried. Oh God, she cried. Wrenching, gut-hurting sobs.

When she finished, she whispered, "I'm sorry."

He huffed a laugh and lifted her chin with one finger. "Make it up to me," he murmured.

She nodded and started to unbutton his shirt. He chuckled again. "No, little cat. It goes like this…" He looked into her eyes and stroked her cheek. "I love you, MacKensie."

Her heart seemed to stop, then compress, then sink. She just stared at him.

A crease appeared in his cheek. "We'll try again. I love you, MacKensie." He raised his eyebrows, waiting for…

He wanted her to—he wanted her to love him back? He *wanted* that? From *her?* She met his gaze, saw the patience and—oh God—the love. "I love you, Alex," she whispered.

His eyes crinkled. "Better. A little tentative, but I'm sure you'll improve with practice. I love you, MacKensie." He waited.

Her lips curved, and she said firmly, "I love you, Alex."

"Perfect." He kissed her, sweetly at first, tenderly, then so possessively that her heart started to pound. His hands moved over her breasts, his thumbs tormenting her nipples into swollen peaks. When he released her, she moaned a complaint.

Smiling, he put her hands on his shirt again. "Now, little sub, now you may show how much you love me."

She undid the buttons, removed his shirt, and settled beside him. Her bottom touched the bed, and she winced and then gave him a mean look. "You want me to show you like you did me?"

He barked a laugh, and suddenly she was underneath him, his weight pressing her down into the mattress. He shoved her legs apart, freed his cock, and slid it into her in one ruthless thrust. One hand fisted in her hair, holding her face in place as he frowned into her eyes. "Little sub, if you try to swat me, I'll tie you up so tight, you won't be able to move." He slid his cock in and out, as if he'd felt the clench of her pussy. "And then I'll take you so many times, you won't be able to walk." In and out.

"Or maybe I'll strap a dildo in you and a vibrator on your front and make you come until your voice goes hoarse."

Her breath stopped, and then she could see the amusement in his eyes that he'd hidden. "Ah, I know. I'll have a party and let everyone spank you"—he lifted her legs, pressing her knees upward, then moved inside her, harder, deeper, faster—"and then I'll take you again."

✧ ✧ ✧ ✧ ✧

Peter led them through the formal parlor and into a more-casual family room before raising his voice. "Hope. Alex and MacKensie are here."

Mac braced herself. She'd had years of seeing disdain on people's faces. Peter had appeared friendly, but hey, he was a lawyer and Alex's friend. He'd never—

Her thoughts blanked when Hope appeared, sped across the room, and wrapped Mac in a whirlwind hug. A hug? After a second of complete shock, Mac managed to lift her arms and hug back. And breathe. Breathing was important.

Eventually Hope stepped back and set her hands on her hips. "So—at the party yesterday? Well, I've never seen anyone retreat that fast before. You were gone before anyone could move." She scowled. "You dummy."

Mac shook her head as her preconceptions slid right out from under her. "Why are you still talking to me? Didn't you hear anything that man said?"

"Yeah. And Alex explained. You were just a baby." Hope's brows drew together. "A couple of my students have dropped out over the years, and I pray they aren't getting caught in something like that." She pointed at the couch. "Sit down and don't even think about trying to escape."

When the pixie trotted back into her kitchen, Mac looked at the men helplessly.

Alex grinned.

Peter ruffled her hair and pushed her toward the living room. "Sit. You have some decisions to make, and Alex asked me to help you with them."

Decisions? Mac sank down on the couch, reassured when Alex sat next to her, his warmth against her side. He leaned back, as always totally at ease, his arms resting on the back of the couch.

Hope emerged from the kitchen with a tray of drinks. "Iced tea. I hope you like it," she said. She set the tray on the coffee table, handed Peter a glass, and then perched on the arm of his chair.

"Thanks, love." Peter smiled at Hope, then tipped his glass at Mac. "Are you planning to stay in Seattle, MacKensie? And will you be with Alex?"

She opened her mouth, closed it, and then burst out, "I can't." She felt Alex stiffen and turned to him, trying to make him see. "You have a reputation. You're one of the movers and shakers in Seattle society. My being with you will ruin your reputation. They'd ostracize you." Her chest hurt, but she forced the words out. "I can't do that to you. Don't you understand?"

Alex glanced at Peter. "See why I love her?" Taking her hand, he kissed her palm. "I am one of the owners of a notorious BDSM club named Chains, and people know that. So I already have a disreputable reputation that, oddly enough, everyone manages to ignore. You will do me no damage, pet."

"Your mother..."

He grinned. "Ah. That you'll have to take up with her, although I think you underestimate her. But, MacKensie, her opinion doesn't affect what is between us."

Didn't he understand anything?

"MacKensie." Peter dragged her attention back. "Assuming none of this happened, would you want to stay with Alex?"

"Oh God, yes."

Alex chuckled and pulled her closer, tucking her into his side as if she were a little chick. "There's the right answer."

"All right." Peter pursed his lips as he thought. "Does Carl Dickerson have anything else to throw at you, or has he shot his wad, so to speak?"

"Peter. Honestly!" Hope smacked him on the thigh.

Mac shook her head. How could they take this so calmly, even joking about it, as if her past was a simple problem to be solved? "There's nothing else. I didn't do drugs, wasn't arrested, didn't steal."

"Just a year of being a baby hooker, then. Good." Peter smiled at her. "Honey, you realize what that means, don't you?"

Mac thought about it. Alex's hand cupped her shoulder, his thumb stroking her skin gently. Patiently. She began to see what Peter was driving at. Dickerson didn't have anything else he could throw at her. He'd already broadcast her past in the highest society and vet circles. "He can't do anything worse than what he's already done."

"Very good." Peter smiled. "I did a little checking. He has a nasty temper—one of the reasons that he's changed clinics several times—but apparently he just had an acrimonious divorce, and his wife made some very unflattering comments about him in public."

Mac bit her lip, smothering a hysterical laugh. Perhaps insulting Dickerson's size and performance had been a bit unwise.

"So, knowing that, the next move is yours. You can cower in the house or simply go on. Your decision, honey."

"He's a vet. I'm bound to run into him again," Mac whispered.

"Probably so."

Mac stared at her hands, the fingers infected with a fine trembling. He would undoubtedly denounce her again. But gossip being what it was, by that time, everyone would already know her past. He could yell...but people had yelled at her before. He could proposition...but she'd dealt with that before too. So yes, he'd done his worst, and she'd survived. Alex was not only still with her but loved her. *I've done enough running and hiding.* Her shoulders straightened. "I'm not going to cower."

✧ ✧ ✧ ✧ ✧

As they were leaving, Alex watched MacKensie give Hope another hug. Much of the tension had left her body; she'd been bracing herself for the pain of losing her friends. He glanced at Peter. "Thank you. She needed an objective viewpoint."

"My pleasure." Peter smiled. "Not that I had a choice. I think Hope has adopted her. We still on for tomorrow afternoon?"

"Yes." Alex nodded. "You'll be able to manage that as well as the party?"

"Oh yes." Peter's eyes glinted with the look he had right before he did a closing argument to the jury. "I'm looking forward to a wonderful evening."

Chapter Twenty-two

Mac stopped in the center of the sidewalk, her feet refusing to move farther. Peter's house glimmered with light. As the sound of lilting music and a multitude of voices wafted out the open door, Mac just knew this was going to be a horrible evening.

Alex halted and looked down at her, but didn't speak. Just waited.

Mac took a breath of the cold night air. Okay. She had to do this. One more trial in an already-very-full day. She shook her head. *Damn Alex anyway.* Late in the afternoon, his friends had shown up at the house for "playtime," and Alex, going into Dom mode, had forced Mac to explain her past. All of it.

Peter and Hope knew, of course, but Hope had a big heart. Apparently so did others.

"Honestly," Tess had said. *"If someone held teenage fiascos against me, I'd be dead meat. Not many of us get through that age without screwing up royally at least once."*

And over the next couple of hours, each Dom had yanked her over his lap and swatted her a few times, telling her that if she needed to know she was cared for, they had the laps and the palms to help her out.

Her bottom still hurt. She glared at Alex, and as if he understood, he slid an arm around her waist, then down, until his hand rubbed her tender butt.

"Jerk," she whispered.

"True." He nuzzled her cheek. "But we all enjoyed it."

She sighed and kissed him lightly. Painful as it had been, they'd actually made her feel cared for. Like in gym class when people lined up on sides... Only this time, she actually had someone standing on *her* side.

After the play session, Hope and Tess had chattered away, taking turns scolding Mac when she got teary-eyed over their continued friendship. They'd insisted on helping Mac dress for this party. Tess had pulled Mac's hair back into a low ponytail, and Hope had applied her makeup. As a result, she looked ten years younger, more like a college student than a professional.

I can do this. Mac gave herself a mental nod and started her legs moving again. *I can do this.* She repeated it all the way up to the door of Peter's brick home. She managed to let the doorman take her coat, although it felt as if she were relinquishing her armor. But she looked good, partly because of the unexpected addition to her wardrobe that had appeared in her closet earlier. The silky blue cocktail dress—true blue, Alex called it—flowed around her legs. The bodice, decorated with darker blue stones, was modest and subdued.

The first sight of the room full of people stopped her in her tracks, and she had to instruct her feet to move—gracefully, dammit—into the room. Beside her, Alex didn't speak, simply walked with her, his arm brushing against hers with every step.

She knew full well that he wanted to walk in front of her and slay the dragons for her. That he'd let her stand on her own as she'd asked was a gift to her. God, she loved him.

They moved into the center of the room. So many people, and she could feel the impact of their eyes. *This is just a party.* She'd been to parties before and even enjoyed herself. *I can do this.*

"Take a breath, little cat," Alex murmured.

When she spotted the man, her stomach dropped to her toes. Why was he here? Surely Peter hadn't invited him. He wouldn't do that to her. She started to shrink like Saran Wrap in a fire.

Alex's fingers lifted her chin so she could meet his uncompromising blue eyes. "When our kitten screws up, does he dwell on it? Even if I scold him, what does he look like?"

This morning, the kitten had knocked over a bowl from the mantel. When Alex scolded him, Chef had given a haughty look and stalked away, tiny tail straight up in the air, indifference in every step.

"I call you 'little cat' for a reason, you know," he murmured. "Even before I knew how well you land on your feet."

Well. She felt her spine straighten and her chin come up. He was right. She'd turned her life around. She deserved respect, not scorn.

"That's it."

And they continued forward.

As Alex greeted friends, Mac kept an eye on Dickerson. Her mouth dropped open when Peter and Hope strolled over to him, all chummy and smiling. After a minute, Peter turned and nodded at Alex, and then the traitorous lawyer actually winked at Mac before continuing his conversation with Dickerson.

Hand on the small of Mac's back, Alex guided her right up to Peter. He didn't even look at Dickerson. "Peter, I wanted to ask you—"

"Alex," Peter interrupted. "Have you met Carl Dickerson? He recently joined your mother's list of vet volunteers."

"Indeed." Alex gave him an indifferent glance, not extending a hand. "Peter, I wanted to ask—"

Dickerson's face purpled at being ignored, and his glare descended on Mac. He obviously thought she'd caused trouble for him. "Nice to see you again, missy. Long way from the alleys, isn't it? How much are you charging these days?"

"Excuse me?" Peter said, lifting his eyebrows.

Dickerson snorted. "Oh, weren't you at the last party? The little lady here used to be a whore back in Des Moines. I think—"

"Really?" Peter interrupted. "How do you know her, then?" His voice had risen to match Dickerson's.

What was he doing? But the murmured "little cat" from Alex kept Mac in place, head high.

"How do you think?" Dickerson gave a filthy laugh. "Hell, she'd do anybody who offered the price. She—"

Victoria appeared on Mac's other side, her voice ice cold and carrying. "Have you ever noticed that men with inadequate equipment are incredibly loud?" She didn't—quite—sniff at Dickerson before looking at Mac. "My dear, how old were you and how long did you do this?"

Starting to get an idea of what was going on, Mac wet her lips. "Fifteen. For a year." She tried, but her voice didn't come out very loud.

It didn't matter. Hope jumped in. Loudly. "Fifteen? Oh my God, you were just a baby."

"Indeed." The look Victoria gave Dickerson could have cut stone. "Please leave. I do not associate with men who prey on youngsters."

Dickerson's mouth dropped open.

Then Alex attacked. "Might I add," he said, and his voice didn't rise, but it carried, "if you ever speak disparagingly about my fiancée again, I will take you apart, physically, financially, and socially"—he cast his mother an amused look—"although the *socially* is probably superfluous at this point."

Dickerson sputtered. "Did you just threaten me?"

"What? Do you lack ears as well as morals?" Victoria did sniff this time.

"Good job, Alex," a man boomed from across the room. "Does she want to press charges?"

Startled, Mac glanced over. Wasn't that the police commissioner?

Bug-eyed, Dickerson stood frozen until Peter leaned forward and said quietly, "Leave. Now." Dom voice.

No one seemed to notice his exit as the room broke out in a fresh buzz of conversation. Expecting to hear her past hashed to pieces, Mac heard people discussing their children and how difficult teenagers were to deal with, the need to clean up the streets and increase the services to the victims. The glances that came her way showed sympathy and even respect.

"That was totally fun," Hope announced, bouncing up and down on her toes. "Can we cut the legs off someone else?"

"Bloodthirsty midget." Peter ruffled her hair and then looked at Mac. "You stood up well. Very nice."

As he and Hope walked into the crowd, Mac pulled in a breath. Dear God, what had she done to deserve such friends?

She turned to Alex and kissed him on the mouth. "You could have warned me, you sadistic bastard."

His lips quirked. "You wouldn't have come."

"I... Yes, probably true," she admitted. "So thank you. But, um...the fiancée thing? Isn't that something people discuss? I've even heard of terms bandied about referring to *proposals?*"

"No," he said. His eyes narrowed. "You will marry me. Refusal is no longer an option." One hand gripping her arm, he kept her pinned in his gaze.

Not that she'd refuse, but he needed to learn that he couldn't walk all over her—except when he was doing his Dom thing. She shivered, thinking of the previous night and...

His lips curved, and his thumb stroked her lips.

"Ahem."

Alex's mother. Still here. Frak me. Mac reddened and tried to step away from Alex.

His grip only tightened. After a long, long second, he released her, making sure she realized it had been his choice, not hers.

Victoria glared at her son before saying, "I fear I need to leave; I have another engagement across town."

When Mac realized why Victoria had come, she had to blink back tears. "I can't thank you enough. You cowed him completely." The memory replaced her tears with an urge to laugh. "It's amazing how you can do that."

"It will be my pleasure to teach you," Victoria said. "And as for thanking me? Since you already have a Butler and now a *Chef*, I believe it's time to start on grandbabies. Brown eyes or blue, dark hair or light—I'm quite flexible."

The idea of having a baby with Alex sent a surge of joy through Mac that she couldn't conceal, and Victoria's smile warmed for a second before she frowned at her son. "*Human* grandbabies, Alex. Human."

Alex chuckled. As his mother walked away, he bent over, his breath warm against Mac's ear. "My mother is not to be denied. So when we return, you will strip and place yourself over the spanking bench to await my pleasure."

Her mouth opened as a wave of heat washed through her.

His finger traced a path down her cheek. "If I am unsatisfied in any way, you will be in the right position for me to show my dissatisfaction."

The thought of his hand slapping against her bottom made her want to squirm, and she realized the thought no longer brought images of unease—just of heat.

His thumb rubbed over her lips as he smiled at her. "I love you, little sub." He waited.

The words came ever so easily this time. "I love you, Alex."

His brows drew together at the omission of the expected *Sir*.

With a sense of growing anticipation, she repeated, slowly, defiantly, "I love you…*Alex*."

His eyes glinted. "I see. Perhaps it's time to sample some of the equipment off the wall." His hand closed over her arm, warm against her bare skin.

Equipment? No. No way. The firm grasp mercilessly holding her in place sent a thrill through her even as she whispered frantically, "*Sir.* I meant *Sir.*"

He smiled at her—*oh frak*—and she knew she was doomed.

~ *The End* ~

Book List by Cherise Sinclair

Masters of the Shadowlands series

Club Shadowlands

Dark Citadel

Breaking Free

Lean on Me

Make Me, Sir

To Command and Collar

This Is Who I Am

If Only

Mountain Masters & Dark Haven series

Master of the Mountain

Doms of Dark Haven 1: Anthology

Master of the Abyss

Doms of Dark Haven 2: Western Night Anthology

My Liege of Dark Haven

The Wild Hunt Legacy series (Erotic paranormal ménage)

Hour of the Lion

Winter of the Wolf

Standalone novels

The Dom's Dungeon

The Starlight Rite (Erotic Sci-Fi romance)

Visit www.CheriseSinclair.com/books/ for book lists and buy links for all books

About the Author

Having to wear glasses in elementary school can scar a person for life. Dubbed a nerd at an early age, Cherise Sinclair has been trying to live up to the stereotype ever since. And what better way than being an author?

Known for writing deeply emotional stories, Cherise is the author of fifteen erotic romance novels, most with a BDSM theme. (Please do not mention the phrase *mommy porn* in her presence.) Called an "ascendant erotica queen" by *Rolling Stone Magazine*, Cherise has a multitude of awards ranging from a National Leather Award to a *Romantic Times* Reviewer's Choice nomination to the GoodReads BDSM group award for best author of 2011.

When not writing, she can be found gardening, arguing with her beloved rascal of a husband, or traveling. And buried under a snoozing cat or two, she's *always* reading—if nothing else is available, she'll read cereal boxes.

Visit Cherise online:

Website:
http://www.CheriseSinclair.com

Goodreads:
www.goodreads.com/author/show/2882485.Cherise_Sinclair

Facebook:
www.facebook.com/CheriseSinclair

Preview of
Masters of the Shadowlands 1:
Club Shadowlands

*Club Shadowlands is a breathtaking BDSM that held my attention till I turned the last page. In one word...*POWERFUL. *Recommended Read ~* Blackraven Reviews

Her car disabled during a tropical storm, Jessica Randall discovers the isolated house where she's sheltering is a private bondage club. At first shocked, she soon becomes aroused watching the interactions between the Doms and their subs. But she's a professional woman—an accountant—and surely isn't a submissive ...is she?

Master Z hasn't been so attracted to a woman in years. But the little sub who has wandered into his club intrigues him. She's intelligent. Reserved. Conservative. After he discovers her interest in BDSM, he can't resist tying her up and unleashing the passion she hides within.

✧ ✧ ✧ ✧ ✧

Excerpt from Club Shadowlands

Jessica shivered as the wind howled through the palmettos and plastered her drenched clothing against her chilled body. Couldn't stop now. Doggedly, she set one foot in front of the other, her waterlogged shoes squishing with every step.

An eternity later, she spotted a glimmer of light. Relief rushed through her when she reached a driveway studded with hanging lights. Surely whoever lived here would let her wait out the storm. She walked through the ornate iron gates, up the palm-lined drive past landscaped lawns, until finally she reached a three-story stone mansion. Black wrought iron lanterns illumined the entry.

"Nice place," she muttered. And a little intimidating. She glanced down at herself to check the damage. Mud and rain streaked her tailored slacks and white button-down shirt, hardly a suitable image for a conservative accountant. She looked more like something even a cat would refuse to drag in.

Shivering hard, she brushed at the dirt and grimaced as it only streaked worse. She stared up at the huge oak doors guarding the entrance. A small doorbell in the shape of a dragon glowed on the side panel, and she pushed it.

Seconds later, the doors opened. A man, oversized and ugly as a battle-scarred Rottweiler, looked down at her. "I'm sorry, miss, you're too late. The doors are locked."

What the heck did that mean?

"P-please," she said, stuttering with the cold. "My car's in a ditch, and I'm soaked, and I need a place to dry out and call for help." But did she really want to go inside with this scary-looking guy? Then she shivered so hard her teeth clattered together, and her mind was made up. "Can I come in? Please?"

He scowled at her, his big-boned face brutish in the yellow entry light. "I'll have to ask Master Z. Wait here." And the bastard shut the door, leaving her in the cold and dark.

Jessica wrapped her arms around herself, standing miserably, and finally the door opened again. Again the brute. "Okay, come on in."

Relief brought tears to her eyes. "Thank you, oh, thank you." Stepping around him before he could change his mind, she barreled into a small entry room and slammed into a solid body. "Oomph," she huffed.

Firm hands gripped her shoulders. She shook her wet hair out of her eyes and looked up. And up. The guy was big, a good six feet, his shoulders wide enough to block the room beyond.

He chuckled, his hands gentling their grasp on her arms. "She's freezing, Ben. Molly left some clothing in the blue room; send one of the subs."

"Okay, boss." The brute—Ben—disappeared.

"What is your name?" Her new host's voice was deep, dark as the night outside.

"Jessica." She stepped back from his grip to get a better look at her savior. Smooth black hair, silvering at the temples, just touching his collar. Dark gray eyes with laugh lines at the corners. A lean, hard face with the shadow of a beard adding a hint of roughness. He wore tailored black slacks and a black silk shirt that outlined hard muscles underneath. If Ben was a Rottweiler, this guy was a jaguar, sleek and deadly.

"I'm sorry to have bothered—" she started.

Ben reappeared with a handful of golden clothing that he thrust at her. "Here you go."

She took the garments, holding them out to keep from getting the fabric wet. "Thank you."

A faint smile creased the manager's cheek. "Your gratitude is premature, I fear. This is a private club."

"Oh. I'm sorry." Now what was she going to do?

"You have two choices. You may sit out here in the entryway with Ben until the storm passes. The forecast stated the winds and rain would die down around six or so in the morning, and you won't get a tow truck out on these country roads until then. Or you may sign papers and join the party for the night."

She looked around. The entry was a tiny room with a desk and one chair. Not heated. Ben gave her a dour look.

Sign something? She frowned. Then again, in this lawsuit-happy world, every place made a person sign releases, even to visit a fitness center. So she could sit here all night. Or...be with happy people and be warm. *No-brainer.* "I'd love to join the party."

"So impetuous," the manager murmured. "Ben, give her the paperwork. Once she signs—or not—she may use the dressing room to dry off and change."

"Yes, sir." Ben rummaged in a file box on the desk, pulled out some papers.

The manager tilted his head at Jessica. "I will see you later then."

Ben shoved three pages of papers at her and a pen. "Read the rules. Sign at the bottom." He scowled at her. "I'll get you a towel and clothes."

She started reading. *Rules of the Shadowlands.*

"Shadowlands. That's an unusual na—" she said, looking up. Both men had disappeared. Huh. She returned to reading, trying to focus her eyes. Such tiny print. Still, she never signed anything without reading it.

Doors will open at...

Water pooled around her feet, and her teeth chattered so hard she had to clench her jaw. There was a dress code. Something about cleaning the equipment after use. Halfway down the second page, her eyes blurred. Her brain felt like icy slush. *Too cold—I can't do this.* This was just a club, after all; it wasn't like she was signing mortgage papers.

Turning to the last page, she scrawled her name and wrapped her arms around herself. *Can't get warm.*

Ben returned with some clothing and towels, then showed her into an opulent restroom off the entry. Glass-doored stalls along one side faced a mirrored wall with sinks and counters.

After dropping the borrowed clothing on the marble counter, she kicked her shoes off and tried to unbutton her shirt. Something moved on the wall. Startled, Jessica looked up and saw a short, pudgy woman with straggly blonde hair and a pale complexion blue with cold. After a second, she recognized herself. *Ew.* Surprising they'd even let her in the door.

In a horrible contrast with Jessica's appearance, a tall, slender, absolutely gorgeous woman walked into the restroom and gave her a scowl. "I'm supposed to help you with a shower."

Get naked in front of Miss Perfection? Not going to happen. "Thanks, b-b-b-but I'm all right." She forced the words past her chattering teeth. "I don't need help."

"Well!" With an annoyed huff, the woman left.

I was rude. Shouldn't have been rude. If only her brain would kick back into gear, she'd do better. She'd have to apologize. Later. If she ever got dried off and warm. She needed dry clothes. But, her hands were numb, shaking uncontrollably, and time after time, the buttons slipped from her stiff fingers. She couldn't even get her slacks off, and she was shuddering so hard her bones hurt.

"Dammit," she muttered and tried again.

The door opened. "Jessica, are you all right? Vanessa said—" The manager. "No, you are obviously not all right." He stepped inside, a dark figure wavering in her blurry vision.

"Go away."

"And find you dead on the floor in an hour? I think not." Without waiting for her answer, he stripped her out of her clothes as one would a two-year-old, even peeling off her sodden bra and panties. His hands were hot, almost burning, against her chilled skin.

She was naked. As the thought percolated through her numb brain, she jerked away and grabbed at the dry clothing. His hand intercepted hers.

"No, pet." He plucked something from her hair, opening his hand to show muddy leaves. "You need to warm up and clean up. Shower."

He wrapped a hard arm around her waist and moved her into one of the glass-fronted stalls behind where she'd been standing. With his free hand, he turned on the water, and heavenly warm steam billowed up. He adjusted the temperature.

"In you go," he ordered. A hand on her bottom, he nudged her into the shower.

The water felt scalding hot against her frigid skin, and she gasped, then shivered, over and over, until her bones hurt. Finally, the heat began to penetrate, and the relief was so intense, she almost cried.

Some time after the last shuddering spasm, she realized the door of the stall was open. Arms crossed, the man leaned against the door frame, watching her with a slight smile on his lean face.

"I'm fine," she muttered, turning so her back was to him. "I can manage by myself."

"No, you obviously cannot," he said evenly. "Wash the mud out of your hair. The left dispenser has shampoo."

Mud in her hair. She'd totally forgotten; maybe she *did* need a keeper. After using the vanilla-scented shampoo, she let the water sluice through her hair. Brown water and twigs swirled down the drain. The water finally ran clear.

"Very good." The water shut off. Blocking the door, he rolled up his sleeves, displaying corded, muscular arms. She had the unhappy feeling he was going to keep helping her, and any protest would be ignored. He'd taken charge as easily as if she'd been one of the puppies at the shelter where she volunteered.

"Out with you now." When her legs wobbled, he tucked a hand around her upper arm, holding her up with disconcerting ease. The cooler air hit her body, and her shivering started again.

After blotting her hair, he grasped her chin and tipped her face up to the light. She gazed up at his darkly tanned face, trying to summon up enough energy to pull her face away.

"No bruises. I think you were lucky." Taking the towel, he dried off her arms and hands, rubbing briskly until he appeared satisfied with the pink color. Then he did her back and shoulders. When he reached her breasts, she pushed at his hand. "I can do that." She stepped back so quickly that the room spun for a second.

"Jessica, be still." Then he ignored her sputters like she would a buzzing fly, his attentions gentle but thorough, even to lifting each breast and drying underneath.

When he toweled off her butt, she wanted to hide. If there was any part of her that should be covered, it was her hips. Overweight. *Jiggly*. He didn't seem to notice.

Then he knelt and ordered, "Spread your legs."

No way. She flushed, didn't move.

He looked up, lifted an eyebrow. And waited. Her resolve faltered beneath the steady, authoritative regard.

She slid one leg over. His towel-covered hand dried between her legs, sending a flush of embarrassment through her. The full enormity of her position swept through her: she was naked in front of a complete stranger, letting him touch her...there. Her breath stopped even as disconcerting pleasure moved through her. But she didn't know him. A tinge of fear made her stiffen.

His gaze lifted, and his eyes narrowed. "Relax, pet. Almost done." He dried then chafed the skin on her legs until she could feel the heat. "There, that should do it."

Ignoring her attempt to take the clothing, he helped her step into a long, slinky skirt that reached midcalf—at least it covered her hips—then pulled a gold-colored, stretchy tank top over her head. His muscular fingers brushed her breasts as he adjusted the fit. He studied her for a moment before smiling slowly. "The clothes suit you, Jessica, far more than your own. A shame to hide such a lovely figure."

Lovely? She knew better, but the words still gave her a glowy feeling inside. She glanced down to check for herself and frowned at the way the low-cut elastic top outlined her full breasts. She could see every little bump in her nipples. *Good grief.* She crossed her arms over her chest.

His chuckle was deep and rich. "Come, the main room is much warmer."

Wrapping an arm around her, he led her out of the bathroom, through the entry, and into a huge room crowded with people. Her eyes widened as she looked around. The club must take up the entire first floor of the house. A circular bar of darkly polished wood ruled the center of the room. Wrought iron sconces cast flickering light over tables and chairs, couches and coffee tables. Plants created small secluded areas. The right corner of the room had a dance floor where music pulsed with a throbbing beat. Farther down, parts of the wall were more brightly lit, but she couldn't see past the crowd to make out why.

Her steps slowed as she realized the club members were attired in extremely provocative clothing, from skintight leathers and latex to corsets to—*oh my*—one woman was bare from the waist up. A long chain dangled from...*clamps* on her nipples.

What in the world? Wincing, Jessica glanced up at her host. "Um, excuse me?" What was his name, anyway?

He stopped. "You may call me Sir."

Like the Marines or something? "Uh, right. Exactly what kind of club *is* this?" Over the music and murmur of voices, a woman's voice suddenly wailed in unmistakable orgasm. Heat flared in Jessica's face.

Amusement glinted in the man's dark eyes. "It's a private club, and tonight is bondage night, pet.

❖ ❖ ❖ ❖ ❖

Made in the USA
San Bernardino, CA
16 January 2014